Meet Urgum – the fiercest savage the Lost Desert has ever known. Catching cannon balls in his mouth, putting cobras down his vest – he's completely mental. But always saving him from disaster is testing the patience of the gods. So, to calm him down, they arrange a 10-year-old daughter for him. And what a barbarian babe Molly turns out to be in this fearsomely funny novel.

Also by Kjartan Poskitt

The *Murderous Maths* series
Isaac Newton and his Apple
The Gobsmacking Galaxy
A Brief History of Pants
The Magic of Pants

URGUM THE AXE MAN

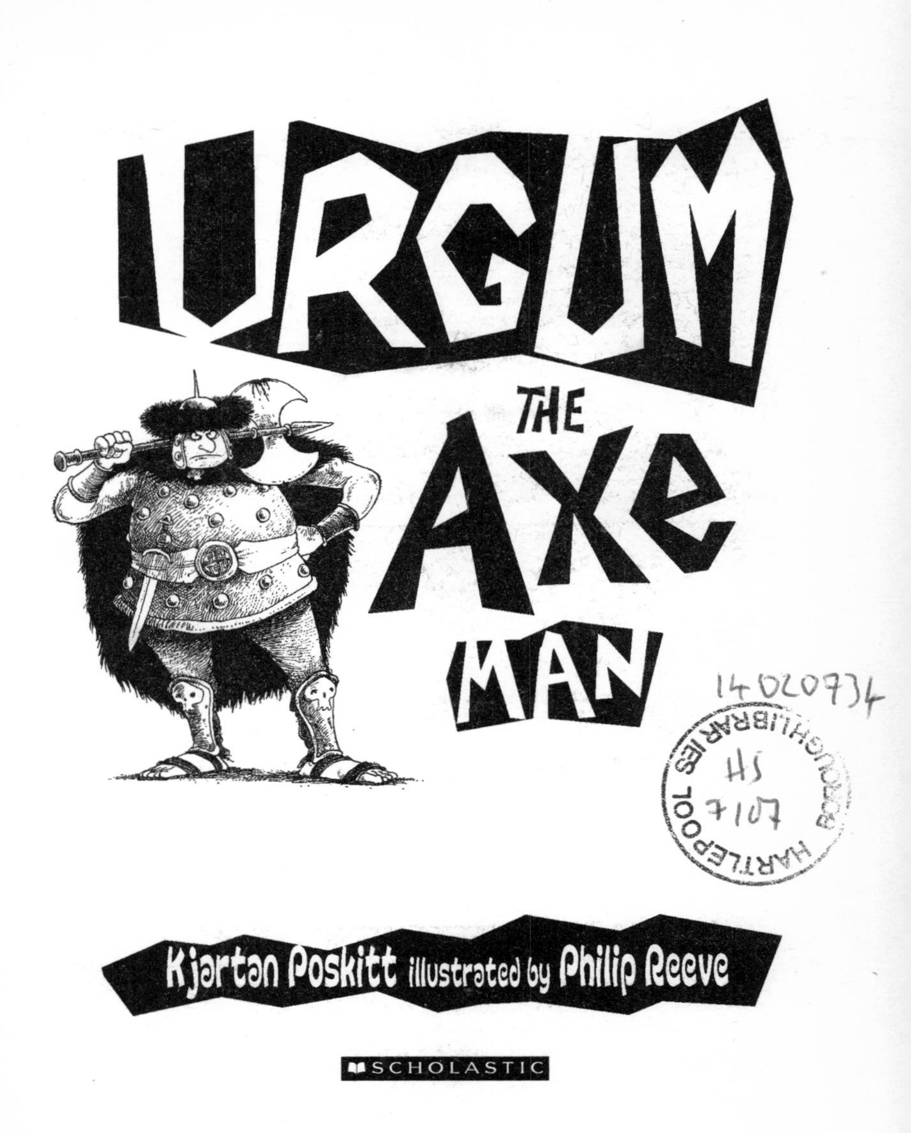

Kjartan Poskitt illustrated by Philip Reeve

SCHOLASTIC

First published in the UK in 2006 by Scholastic Children's Books
An imprint of Scholastic Ltd
Euston House, 24 Eversholt Street, London, NW1 1DB, UK
Registered office: Westfield Road, Southam, Warwickshire, CV47 0RA

This edition published by Scholastic Ltd, 2007

10 digit ISBN 1 407 10257 5
13 digit ISBN 978 1407 10257 3

A CIP catalogue record for this book is available from the British Library

Printed in the UK by CPI Bookmarque, Croydon, CR0 4TD
Papers used by Scholastic Children's Books are made from wood grown in sustainable forests.

1 3 5 7 9 10 8 6 4 2

www.scholastic.co.uk/zone

For Bridget and
our four Mollys

PART ONE

THE RETURNING HERO

PART TWO

WHEN THINGS CHANGED

PART THREE

THE FOOTPRINT IN THE FLOWER BED

PART FOUR

THE TAX WARS

the Lost Desert
Some mountains
Golgarth Cragg
The Old Tar Pit
Sacrifice Tree
Smiley Alley
Giant Juppotan
Track of t
The Wandering Jungle
N
E
W
S
Here be Dragons!

LAPLACE PALACE
The Singing Pool
Shoo-boo-be-doop
The PECULIAR STAIN
A Confused Bush
Some more mountains
Wandering Jungle
The FORGOTTEN CRATER
Here Be Unicorns
Here Bee NAPPARS
The Unsightly Hills of NAPP
KEY
Swampy bits
Woods
Gritty bits
Rude dwellings
Pointy bits
Biscuit crumbs

PART ONE
The Returning Hero
The LOST DESERT

The Watchers in the Sky

The dust of the Lost Desert streamed out in a cloud behind the horses thundering around the brim of the Forgotten Crater and on towards Golgarth Cragg. Evil cries echoed across the dry plains, rock lizards cowered in the shadows, a rattlesnake hastily buried itself in the hot sand and a scorpion scuttled to hide in the roots of a giant yellow cactus. Even the bloated milligobs crawling over a donkey skull froze and held their breath, praying for the barbarian riders to pass by. The heavy figure on the leading horse was waving a massive axe

around his head so recklessly it was a miracle that it hadn't hacked any chunks out of the sweating beast's lurching neck. White sunlight glinted off the axeman's sharpened teeth and the muscles bulging from his arms were as thick and tight as tree roots. It was many years since he had first been sewn into his thick leather breastplate and the slashes and stains on it were a testament to all the many acts of savagery it had witnessed since. His speed and skill with the axe were legendary, his reputation for close-combat fighting was awesome, his treatment of enemies utterly ruthless and his greed at meal times was the subject of ballads. No wonder Urgum the Axeman was the fiercest savage that the Lost Desert had ever known.

"YARGHHH!"

shouted Urgum happily.

Despite all his fantastic abilities and achievements, for Urgum, the main pleasures of life came from the simple things and if there was one thing he liked more than anything else it was galloping madly across the desert with his seven sons, shouting pointlessly. They had been

out at the Unicorn Hunt, and like all good barbaric social events it had involved fighting, bragging, brawling, partying and completely losing track of the time. The one thing it hadn't involved was actually catching any unicorns but they weren't going to let a small detail like that upset their fun as they galloped home to the cragg.

"Yarghhh!" shouted Urgum again. "Wouldn't you agree lads?"

"Yarghhh!" agreed the seven sons.

Urgum's chest swelled with pride. This was GREAT!

Nobody else in the desert would dare to gallop along the thin ledge that ran around the brim of the Forgotten Crater. Behind him the boys had started up their favourite battle chant:

"Are we scared?
NO!
Do we care?
NO!
We're completely
MENTAL!"

Leaning over the side of his horse, Urgum looked straight down to where the rocky path came to a sharp edge and disappeared inches from the pounding hooves. Through the sulphur fumes he could just make out the blood-red glow of the lava lake half a mile below. His horse only had to take one false step and they would tumble together to a ghastly death.

"Are we scared?
NO!

Do we care?

NO!

We're completely

MENTAL!"

Urgum was never worried about suffering a ghastly death for one simple reason: he was a true barbarian. He knew that if he died really horribly but was utterly fearless about it, he would impress the barbarian gods so much that he would be rewarded in the afterlife with a seat at the high table in the Hallowed Halls of Sirrus. In fact, if one thing did bother Urgum, it was the thought that he might die quietly in his sleep with a happy little smile on his face and – his biggest waking fear – his thumb in his mouth. That's why he never missed a chance to risk his life in the most ridiculous and diabolical ways possible.

There was also another reason why Urgum wasn't worried. Quite simply, he hadn't died yet. It didn't seem to matter what mind-numbingly dangerous situation he threw himself into, somehow he always survived. To Urgum it was obvious why – the gods needed him alive. If anything happened to him there wouldn't be anyone else half as good to uphold the proud traditions of fearless savagery ... oh, unless any of his sons managed to become as fierce and fearless as he was. Ho ho, big joke.

This mad charge around the crater would show what they were made of. True, the seven sons were still keeping up with him but, despite their shouts and chants, they looked terrified. Urgum grinned, thinking back to his early savage years, and tried to remember what being scared felt like. In those days, he'd played the normal childish games, like knotting a pair of rattlesnakes together or running along the tightrope over the bear pit, but he would always mutter a quick prayer to his gods to deliver him safely.

At first, he'd worried that he might catch the gods at a bad time, when they weren't listening, or were in a grumpy mood, but gradually he'd got used to the fact that however often he tempted fate, the gods would always save him. After all, the gods had saved and protected his father Urgurt every single time, except when they didn't save him and he died a ghastly death. But if you didn't count that one time (and Urgum didn't because it was only the once), then the gods had always saved Urgurt and would always save Urgum.

Looming ahead of the riders was a thick yellow

sulphur-cloud. From behind him, Urgum could hear the boys desperately muttering prayers for luck, but he didn't bother. The gods wouldn't dare let anything happen to him, and if they did ... well, he'd soon be sitting at their high table eating as much divine food as he could shovel into his face for all eternity. Yum!

They all charged headlong into the cloud, singing:

"ARE WE SCARED?

NO!

DO WE CARE?

NO!

WE'RE COMPLETELY

MENTAL!"

As the eyes of the riders and horses burnt with acidic tears, it became impossible to see the narrow path.

"What do we do now, Urgum?" shouted Ruff, the eldest son, through the yellow mist. "We can't tell where we're going!"

"We ride FASTER of course!" screamed Urgum.

"YARGHHH!"

* * *

Urgum was enjoying himself so much that it would never have occurred to him that up and away in the Hallowed Halls of Sirrus his behaviour was starting to become extremely tedious. Sirrus was where all the spirits of the Lost Desert lived, including the barbarian twin gods Tangor and Tangal. Like any other gods, the divine twins depended on mortal faith for their existence so it was lucky they had Urgum who believed in them absolutely. Unluckily for them Urgum hadn't grasped the real reason why they kept saving his life.

As Urgum led his sons head-first into the sulphur fumes, Tangal was frantically waking her brother from an afternoon nap.

"Look at Urgum!" she said. "He's charging blindly round the edge of the Forgotten Crater."

"So what?" Her brother yawned.

"So the idiot's trying to kill himself again!"

"Oh no! Why does he keep doing that?"

"You know why," said Tangal. "He wants to be seated at our table, eating for eternity."

"But we only just got rid of his father!" said Tangor. "It was fifteen years before he'd had enough, and we still haven't finished the washing up."

"I told you, you should never have let Urgurt die in the first place."

"But he was elephant-wrestling! How stupid can you get? He had to die, it taught him a valuable lesson."

"It taught me a lesson as well," snapped Tangal. "We don't want any more dead savages inviting themselves to our table! And besides, Urgum's the last of the true barbarians."

"What's that got to do with it?"

"If he dies then we'll have no true believers left," explained Tangal. "And if nobody believes in us then we won't be gods any more. We'll just be waiters feeding him at our table for ever and ever. All the other spirits will laugh at us."

Tangor blinked. *What a miserable depressing thought,* he thought.

"Well?" said Tangal. "Do something!"

So Tangor reached a massive hand down through the sulphur-cloud and held a great fingertip by the inside edge of the crater. Just in time, he felt a tingling sensation from the tiny horse hooves as the convoy charged off the edge of the crater and started to run along his finger. He raised the finger up to his face and studied the figures galloping through the mist.

"This is the VERY last time, Urgum," Tangor said, without much conviction.

"We must do something to make him settle down and grow up a bit," said Tangal.

With a sigh, Tangor lowered his finger to the ground a safe distance from the crater and waited until the last horse had charged off and away. Behind him Tangal was rummaging in a box.

"Found it!" she exclaimed.

She held up a curious device that at first glance looked like an ancient hourglass. It was made of an upright brass framework supporting two glass bulbs connected by a narrow neck. The lower bulb was almost full of very fine blue sand and the upper bulb was empty, but the odd feature that made this hourglass different was the unexpected third bulb connected to the back of the neck. This extra bulb was black, making it impossible to see whether it was full or empty.

"The time shifter?" said Tangor. "How will that change Urgum?"

"It'll give us time to arrange a little surprise for him when he gets home."

"Like an ambush?" said Tangor. "Have him surrounded by a whole army, and make him surrender?"

"Surrender?" Tangal snorted. "Urgum? He's our barbarian champion! It'd take more than an army to make him surrender. He'd fight until his axe melted, then he'd punch until his fists melted, then he'd kick until his feet melted and then ... well then he'd die and *then* he'd come up here and sit at our table and eat until his teeth melted. Oh no, to calm Urgum down will take something with a lot more power than an army."

"So what's more powerful than an army?" asked Tangor.

"Honestly!" Tangal chuckled. "You men have no idea at all, have you?" She turned the time shifter over and placed it on the table. Very slowly, the blue sand started to trickle from the top bulb, but the lower bulb remained empty. The grains of time were disappearing into the third, black bulb leaving mortal days, months and even years completely unaccounted for.

Down in the land of the mortals, Urgum emerged from the sulphur-cloud, rubbing his eyes, while beneath him his horse snorted and coughed and finally came to a standstill.

"Wow!" said Urgum as he shook his head to clear it. "Wasn't that just ...

WOW?"

The horse looked around to see who Urgum was talking to, but they were alone. The horse quite reasonably assumed Urgum was talking to him, but not being used to conversation, he wasn't sure how to reply. What should he say? He carefully composed a speech: "You call that 'Wow'? You great sweaty lump. You should try running over jagged rocks through an acid cloud carrying a fat moron on your back sometime. I'll give you 'wow', you stinky lice-ridden hooligan." The horse thought that sounded about right. It was nicely structured, it set the correct tone and delivered his views perfectly. *OK, Urgum,* he decided, *scrape out your ears and get ready for this...*

But just then the other horses and riders staggered from the cloud.

"Wow!" shouted Urgum. "Eh lads? Wow?"

They all cheered.

"So, let's see if you all made it," said Urgum. "Robbin, Ruff, Ruinn, Rakk n' Rekk, Raymond. Hurrah! Let's go."

"Hold it!" said Ruinn counting. "One, two, three, four, five, six."

"Great!" said Urgum. "Let's go."

"But isn't there supposed to be seven of us?"

"Nah!" said Urgum. "That fancy mathematics of yours must be wrong."

A final rider stumbled out of the cloud.

"Told you," said Ruinn.

"Oh!" said Urgum. "Fancy me forgettin' er, thingy ... oh you know who I mean ... whatsisface... "

"The Other One?" asked Ruinn.

"Yeah, him," said Urgum. "Right, let's go. Follow me boys!"

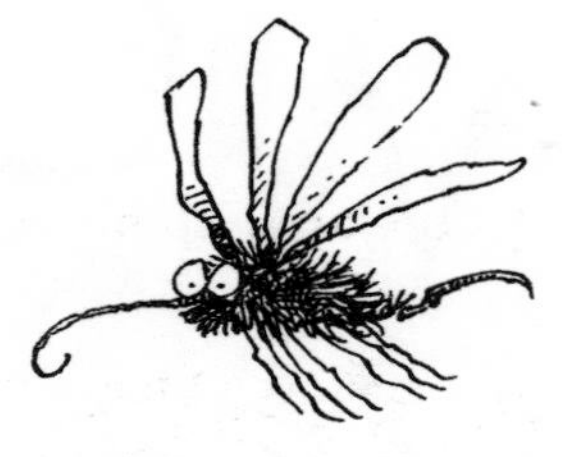

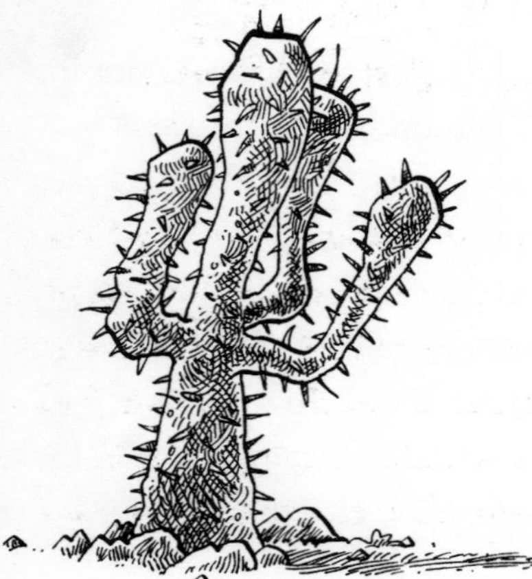

The Boy in the Bags

Urgum reared up his horse, did a mighty cheer of

"YARGHHH!"

and charged off with the sons all following in line. First they all went round in a big circle, then they went round in a smaller circle. Then they did a figure-of-eight and some loops. Finally Urgum slowed down and led them round in smaller and smaller circles until they ended up in the middle with all the horses bumping their noses together at once. Urgum glanced about blankly. The sulphur-cloud had completely dispersed and yet there was no sign of the crater.

"Something the matter, Urgum?" asked Ruinn.

"I just had a great idea," said Urgum. "Ruff, how would you like to lead for a change?"

Ruff was Urgum's number one son and, just in case anyone didn't realize how important he was, he always dressed himself up to look exactly like his father, despite only being half his size. That way he felt confident that one day he would be destined for greatness and glory, but in the meantime he took the job of leading his brothers home very seriously. Unfortunately they didn't take him seriously at all.

"You can depend on me, Father," announced Ruff. He straightened his back and stuck his jaw out. "All right men, prepare to follow me. I am your leader."

The others all gathered around him and sniggered.

"Off you go then, leader," said Ruinn, the second son, the skinny one with the long nose, long chin, long ears and long fingers.

"Right," said Ruff. "I'm going. But remember, nobody else is allowed to go in front of me because I'm the leader."

"Get leading then!" shouted the other sons.

"Certainly," said Ruff uncertainly. "Er ... which way is it, Father?"

"Ha ha!" chanted the twins Rekk and Rakk. "What a loser!"

"He's not just a loser." Ruinn grinned. "He's lost."

Ruff turned on them and pulled his toughest meanest face, which of course made him look sillier than ever. All the others howled with nasty laughter.

"It's not my fault!" bleated Ruff. "It's HIS fault we're lost."

They all looked at Urgum who was pretending that he knew what was going on.

"Me?" said Urgum. "I'm not lost."

"Oh?" said Ruinn, boredly twiddling a long finger into his long ear hole. "So where are you then?"

Urgum leapt from his horse and pointed at the ground beneath his feet.

"I'm HERE. Right lads?"

They all groaned.

"A barbarian always knows where he is!" said Urgum.

"OK." Ruinn sighed. He pulled his long finger out of his ear and examined it. When he spoke again it was unclear whether he was speaking to Urgum or the finger. "We all know where we are, but which way's home?"

"That's more like it," agreed Urgum. "We know where we are, it's the cragg that's got lost. All we have to do is find it."

"I've had enough of this." Ruinn slithered down from his horse. "Golgarth can't be too far away."

"I didn't say you could get down," complained Ruff.

Ruinn ignored him and walked towards a horse which didn't seem to have a rider. Instead, it had a selection of bulging bags tied around the saddle.

Ruinn reached a bony hand into one and fumbled around. "I'm borrowing Raymond's brain."

"Yeah!" said the sons.

"No!" A voice came from inside another of the bags. But Raymond knew he hadn't much choice. His life had been distinctly awkward since he'd stumbled into a pit of razor snakes and been sliced up into forty-seven separate pieces.

He could have been killed if he hadn't had the sense to pray out loud to the gods for deliverance as he fell. This put the gods in an awkward position because Urgum heard him. If they hadn't kept Raymond alive, Urgum might have thought they didn't exist and so he would have stopped believing in them, and then *they* wouldn't have existed any more. That's why Raymond was still around all these years later, but although he'd got used to being in separate bags, he was looking forward to the day when he could stand up in one piece and throw a punch without his fist falling off.

In their way, the brothers were good to him. Robbin especially always took care to make sure his nose was in a different bag to his feet, and that his eyes weren't crossed. When they set out on the Unicorn Hunt, Raymond had volunteered to stay at home but his father wouldn't hear of it.

"Don't be such a baby," Urgum said to the bag that had his ears in it. "It's only a couple of scratches. Besides, if we get a unicorn, we can use the hairs in the tail to stitch you up. It's amazing what you can do with a unicorn's tail."

This caused hysterical laughter amongst the boys. Everybody knew that unicorns were antisocial, snorting, stinking, spike-skulled vermin and the only amazing thing

about a unicorn's tail was that it could survive being dangled over a unicorn's bottom. A single gassy release from the back of a unicorn could poison every living thing for miles around, so it was no wonder the estate managers of the Laplace Palace paid a cash bounty for every unicorn captured with a large cork stuffed in the end. That's why the boys found it a bit hard to believe that being stitched up with a unicorn's tail was the only cure for total bodily dismemberment. Even Raymond found it hard to believe, but it hadn't stopped him hoping.

As the days and nights of the hunt had passed, Raymond realized that they weren't going to catch any unicorns, so instead he started looking forward to getting home and spending some time spread out in the open air rather than just having his body parts jangling about in saddlebags. What he certainly hadn't been looking forward to was having someone's dirty hand fumbling around inside his head bits bag.

"What's Ruinn doing?" asked Ruff.

"He's being clever," said Urgum admiringly as Ruinn pulled out Raymond's brain and placed it on an exposed rock. "All of you, get back and hide."

The only thing to hide behind was a small cactus, and soon all of them and their horses were trying to hide behind it. Before long, two tiny ragged shapes appeared high up in the distant sky.

"There they are!" whispered Ruinn. "I thought it would work."

"What is it?" said Robbin, the largest son. "It just looks like two black dots."

"Shhh!" said the others.

"But why have we got to be quiet for two black dots?" persisted Robbin.

"Quiet!" said Urgum.

"I still can't see why we have to be quiet for two black dots..."

"I'll make you quiet!" Rekk pulled a long dagger out from the pocket on his side.

"Dad!" said Robbin. "Rekk's going to stick a dagger in me!"

"So long as you do it quietly!" hissed Urgum.

"Hey, that's my dagger!" shouted Rakk, reaching across for it. "I was looking for that. Give it here."

"You lent it to me, remember?" Rekk held it out of Rakk's reach.

"Well I want it back now," said his twin.

"But I'm using it to kill Robbin."

"Well just strangle him instead."

"I need you to help me strangle him!" said Rekk.

"I'll only help if I can have my dagger back," said Rakk.

"Dad, Rakk and Rekk are going to strangle me now!" wailed Robbin.

"Be quiet!" said Ruff. "I'm the leader and that's an order."

"Woooo!" said Rekk and Rakk.

Ruff moaned. "Father! Everybody's ignoring me."

"Oi! Behave, the lot of you!" snapped Urgum. "Get behind the cactus, shut up, keep down and watch."

Eventually, the pushing and shoving stopped and they all concentrated on the two ragged shapes as they slowly circled ever closer to the ground.

"See?" Ruinn grinned. "It's our pet vultures Djinta and Percy. I knew Raymond's brain would attract them. As soon as they realize it's alive they'll leave it and head off home again. Get ready to follow them!"

"Me first," said Ruff. "Remember I'm still the leader."

Djinta landed beside the brain. She sniffed it. It smelt too fresh. Percy came down and strutted across to have a look. It seemed too warm. Still, it would be a shame to

waste it. Percy stuck his beak into the brain.

In a flurry of dirty feathers the vultures hurried skywards. No way were they going to eat live meat. Eagles might like the feel of food trying to wriggle its way back up out of their throats, but vultures are far more sophisticated. Disappointed, Percy and Djinta set off back to their perches high on Golgarth Cragg. Far below, Urgum leapt on to his horse and raced after them.

"Come on boys, keep up!" he shouted, as the others followed.

Something Sick and Unnatural

The vultures led Urgum and his sons racing over parched stream beds and under towering rock stacks. They leapt gaping chasms and fallen boulders. Their skins were ripped by thorny cacti and firedart shrubs, sand whipped into their eyes and stone-flies splattered across their teeth. But all too soon, the fun was over and the vultures had come down to perch on a massive burnt-out tree with a selection of skeletons chained around it. The riders galloped up to it and stopped.

"They've led us to the Sacrifice Tree." Urgum panted breathlessly.

"Good old Sacrifice Tree!" The sons cheered.

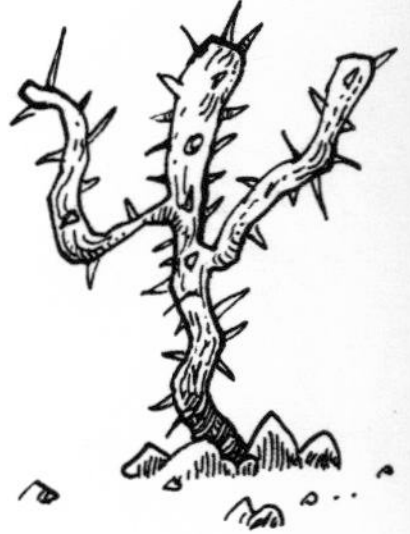

"We'll soon be home again! Here's where we turn off towards Smiley Alley."

"Whoopee!"

The horses headed down the path between two rows of stakes, each of which had a skull nailed to it. As Urgum galloped past, a tear welled up in his eye, for every single one of those skulls brought back fond memories. In the distance, iron-spiked boulders balanced on the high ridge over the entrance to the cragg, and sun-bleached bones crackled beneath the horses' hooves.

"There it is, lads!" cried Urgum. "It's the good old cragg!"

"Good old cragg!" echoed the boys.

"Good old Smiley Alley!"

"Good old Smiley Alley!"

"And there's the good old tar hole where we drowned your uncle Serpus!" shouted Urgum.

"Good old tar hole!"

"And there's the good old flower bed!" screamed Urgum excitedly.

"Good old ... FLOWER BED?"

Urgum yanked his reins, bringing his horse to an abrupt halt.

The sons hadn't had time to pull on their reins. They all smacked straight into the back of Urgum's horse, and Urgum was lobbed right out of his saddle, over the horse's head and landed with a fat thud on his belly.

Groaning, he raised his head and came face to face with a small sand pansy.

"What are you doing here?" he asked the little flower

suspiciously. "That's our cragg and this is our land and you're trespassing."

"He's talking to a little flower," whispered Ruinn to the others, sniggering.

"What?" asked Raymond from inside his saddlebag.

"Urgum's talking to a flower!" Ruinn sniggered again.

"That's a bit scary," said Raymond. "I'm glad my eyes are in a different bag so I don't have to see that."

Urgum had got to his feet and stepped back from the flower.

"Keep well clear, lads!" he said. "Something sick and unnatural has happened here while we've been out. Get back on your horses and prepare for anything."

Every axe, sword, spear and dagger was drawn. Urgum and the sons all bunched together tightly as they advanced past the flower bed. They looked like a giant twenty-eight-legged porcupine.

Look those idiots, thought the sand pansy. *And to think they've got the nerve to call* me *sick...*

The Guardian of Golgarth

Very cautiously, the eight riders edged past the flower bed and on down the path. They turned the final corner towards the rock face and then saw a lone figure standing in the mouthway of the cragg.

"There's Olk!" shouted Urgum. "Good old Olk! He's still exactly where we left him!"

"Phew!" The seven sons sighed with relief.

"Hi, Olk!" Urgum called out. "We're back!"

Even in the shadow of the giant cragg, Olk the sentry looked monstrous. Although his rusty chain-mail vest and ragged leather kilt were both the size of bed sheets, they only just succeeded in covering his upper

chest and lower body, leaving a wide stripe of bulky midriff exposed. His hardened skin was as craggy as the rocks he was guarding, heavy iron bracelets around his upper arms strained to contain his mighty biceps and the cracked toenails stuck out from his bare feet like a row of ostrich beaks. At some distant point in the past an axe had been driven into the top of his skull and the resulting scar ran right over the top of his scalp, dividing his matted hair into two wild clumps. Beneath his spiked eyebrows, his eyes were set so deep inside his head that from his point of view it must have been like looking out of a cave, but all these were just minor details. The most awesome thing about Olk was the weapon he carried.

Slung across his shoulder was the longest and foulest blade in the province. It was rumoured to have beheaded an elephant with one swipe. Even if it had just been leaning up against the wall, Olk's sword would have commanded respect, and in the hands of the Golgarth sentry it demanded no less than total obedience.

As the horses approached the massive figure, they slowed and then stopped.

"We're back, Olk!" said Urgum proudly. "It's us."

Flies buzzed around the crusty smears on the sword, but the heavy face didn't flinch.

"Is she home?" Urgum enquired in a slightly more cautious voice. Behind him the boys all held their breath. They knew that however savage the fighting, bragging and brawling had been on the hunt, by far the scariest part of the trip was wondering what sort of welcome they'd get when they arrived back.

Urgum's "she" was his wife Divina and for some reason that Urgum never understood, she wasn't terribly keen to go on Unicorn Hunts that involved fighting, bragging, brawling, partying and completely losing track of the time. It was a shame because Urgum rather liked his wife and would have been pleased if she'd come along. He wasn't sure how good she'd be at the actual fighting, but certainly her bragging and brawling were well up to the required standard. She also had one extra skill that Urgum couldn't match at all. Although Urgum the Axeman was the undisputed champion of the fearsome double-headed battleaxe and thought nothing of blindfolded one-against-three combat, even he was rendered helpless and pathetic by Divina's mastery of the left eyebrow. All she had to do was catch him with that stony unblinking gaze of hers for a moment, then with one sarcastic lift of that lethal brow his knees would buckle, his lip would quiver and he would be gibbering embarrassed apologies and feeling utterly worthless.

Of course, Divina never tried to stop Urgum going on party hunts – it would have been like trying to stop a thunderstorm from thundering – but when he came back he was never sure how well he would be received. A big happy smile, a few admiring glances at his new scars and "Did you have a lovely time, dear?" would have been nice, but that never happened. The trouble was that Divina had completely the wrong attitude towards things like catching cannonballs in your mouth and putting cobras down your vest. Quite naturally, Urgum regarded these as brave and heroic challenges, but Divina just sniffed and said it was childish showing off.

Even when Urgum had only been away on the briefest of trips, he knew he'd be met with a raised eyebrow on return. Oddly enough, the further it was raised then the less he minded. A really high eyebrow was almost funny, as if she was saying "Oh well, I suppose boys will be boys," but if it was only a tiny movement then it meant he was truly in the pig house.

Urgum hated the power that Divina's eyebrow had on him so he tended to delay coming back, sometimes staying out all night or even a couple of nights or even longer ... but the longer he put it off, the smaller the eyebrow movement would be.

Urgum peered past Olk through the mouthway of the cragg. On the other side of the wall was a giant sandy-bottomed rock basin. In the middle was a large flat open space where a pair of domestic ostriches were peacefully dismembering a piglet under a tree. All around the edge, the high cragg wall was dotted with dark cave entrances, but no one seemed to be about. Urgum's cave was directly opposite the mouthway and he stared at it, hoping to see some sign of movement within, but there was just a cold, unfriendly, unmoving nothing.

Urgum tried to calculate the amount of eyebrow movement to expect and so for the first time since they had set out, he wondered exactly how long they'd been away. It was useless. With a sinking heart he realized the eyebrow was only going to do the minutest twitch. There was nothing else for it, he'd have to put on the jolly face and pretend it wasn't happening.

"She'll be glad to see us," remarked Urgum to Olk

unconvincingly. "Although I expect she's been wondering where we got to because to be honest we're a bit later than we said we were going to be. Still, at least we're all back so we're one big happy family together again, eh Olk?"

No reaction.

"Look what I got for her, a nice bag of pearls and rubies! I won them in a who-can-stick-their-tongue-in-a-candle-flame-longest competition. What do you think, Olk? I bet she can't wait to get her hands on them. So, anyway, it's great to see you and it's been lovely talking to you, Olk, but we'll both be in trouble if we stand here chatting all day. In we go then, lads..."

An eyelid flickered on Olk's heavy face. His lips parted slightly and a solitary word rumbled from the deep inner tubes of his gut.

"PASSWORD."

"But Olk, it's me!" said Urgum. Then he turned to his sons. "Good old Olk, he's a right joker, isn't he, boys?"

The seven sons laughed uncertainly. The idea of an Olk joke was more than scary. They knew that one sweep of his blade could decapitate them all in an instant.

"Password," rumbled Olk.

"Olk, I don't need to say the password because I live here, remember?" explained Urgum. "And since we're good mates, I'll confess a little secret. This'll make you laugh. To be honest ... I've forgotten it."

It didn't make Olk laugh. It made Olk twitch the blade just enough to send the flies off in a panic. All the horses took one step backwards.

"Come on, lads!" said Urgum not daring to turn away from Olk. "Help me here! What was the password?"

There was a muttering of ignorance.

"Oh come on, let's just ask Raymond," said Ruinn. "He'll know." He fumbled around in Raymond's bags until he found an ear. "Hey, Raymond. Can you remember the password?"

"It's Gorefest, isn't it?" said Raymond, from another bag.

"Of course!" Urgum laughed. "That's it! OK, Olk, we've got it! The password is Gorefest. What is it, boys?"

"Gorefest!" they all shouted triumphantly.

"See?" said Urgum. "We knew it all the time. We'll even sing it if you like. Come on lads, one two three..."

"Gorefest, Gorefest, Gorefest..."

"WRONG."

The massive blade rose from Olk's shoulder and prepared to sweep in a large arc at precisely neck height. The horses all took another step backwards. But then Urgum's horse realized that if he hadn't moved the blade would have missed him and hit Urgum, so it took two steps forwards again.

Ruinn was still holding Raymond's ear. He whispered into it.

"You got the password wrong!"

"No I didn't," said the voice in the saddlebag.

"You did!" hissed Ruinn into the ear. "We'll be diced to bits!"

"Big deal," replied Raymond. "Join the club."

Urgum was starting to worry. First there had been the disappearing crater, then the flower bed and now he had the wrong password. Even more worrying, his horse seemed to be nudging him ever closer to that blade. He knew that behind him his sons were all watching so if he backed away now he would die of dishonour, yet if he stayed where he was he would die of dissection. Being a true barbarian he knew that he would rather die than die, so he opted to die. Unless...

"Get back boys," Urgum said to his sons. "Get well

out of it. I've got to face this alone."

The seven sons didn't need telling twice. Without wasting time turning their horses around, they galloped backwards round the corner until they were well out of sight and hearing distance of the entrance.

"I can't believe our dad's taking on Olk!" said Ruff. "I'm so proud to have known him."

"Us too," said the other sons. "He was like a father to us."

"Don't get soft, lads," said Ruinn. "That's not what he'd have wanted and besides we're missing the main point: who gets his stuff when he's dead?"

"I want his axes," said Ruff.

"OK," agreed Ruinn. "So long as I get that diamond dagger of his."

"I want his boots," said Rakk.

"But they'll fit me better!" said Rekk.

"But I can run faster than you," said Rakk.

"Stoppit, stoppit!" shouted Robbin. "Our father is about to die horribly! Do you really think this the best time to argue about his things?"

The others looked at each other in surprise, then shrugged.

"Well of course it is," they replied.

Meanwhile, back by the mouthway of the cragg, Urgum braced himself. Thank goodness his sons weren't going to see what was about to happen. Axes, swords and clubs were futile against the might of Olk. Urgum knew he was going to hate himself for this but he had no choice. Climbing down from his horse and grabbing the bag of pearls and rubies, he cleared his throat then called past Olk across to the entrance to his cave, "Darling! I'm home!"

Nauseous rumbling sounds came from deep within Olk's guts. The blade wavered slightly. Urgum quickly looked around to check his sons were safely gone, then taking a deep gulp, he called again:

"Oh sweetie poppet, it's your little Urgie!"

"...LITTLE URGIE ... LITTLE URGIE ... LITTLE URGIE..."

Urgum felt himself blush as his voice echoed around the inner walls of the cragg. Olk was turning a pale grey colour, his eyes were watering and a strange gagging sound came from his throat. As much as Urgum hated doing it, this was the only safe way to disarm him. He waved the bag of jewels.

"Does Urgie's little honey bundle want her present then? Big Urgie Purgie bear hath been mithing hith likkoo pwetty thuggar lipth..."

"...LIKKOO PWETTY THUGGAR LIPTH ... PWETTY THUGGAR LIPTH ... THUGGAR LIPTH..."

A sour voice came from inside the cave. "And little pretty sugar lips has been missing her big Urgie bear!"

As Olk keeled over to throw up, the blade fell to the ground with a massive crash which brought Urgum's sons running round. They looked on, amazed.

"One good thump to the belly," explained Urgum, rubbing his knuckles. "You've just got to catch the right spot."

And before he had to say any more, his wife stepped from the cave and came over to stand in the mouthway of the cragg. He took a deep breath to prepare himself for the trouble that he knew was coming, but in the split instant before anything else happened, he congratulated himself on marrying her. She was fabulous.

The Savage and the Softhand 1

Unlike Urgum, Divina had not been born a barbarian. Her family were quite the opposite, she had been raised as a softhand: one of the educated people; the readers and writers, the historians. As Urgum had remarked on first meeting her father, Gastan, the softhands were the boring people that never actually DID anything – they just talked about what other people like the barbarians did, and usually moaned about how badly they'd done it. (Even though Gastan hadn't fully agreed with Urgum on this point, he didn't mention it because at the time, he'd a bag of gold coins jammed in his mouth.)

The day they'd met had started normally enough.

Gastan was the chief controller of the Laplace Palace Library and as a special treat he had allowed Divina to accompany him to watch some of the copying scribes being whipped for making punctuation mistakes. The sun was high and they were riding along on their sedan sofa carried by six burly slaves, when up ahead they spotted Urgum standing in the middle of the path, arguing with his horse.

"I don't like the look of him," Gastan said. "Slaves, draw your swords and be prepared to die for us if he gets insolent."

With a resigned sigh, the slaves pulled their swords from their belts and continued carrying the sedan sofa towards Urgum.

"What's this about then?" asked Urgum on seeing them. "How come you've all suddenly got your little swords out?"

"Just a precaution," Divina's father muttered, smearing a bit of cooling cream on his lips with his little finger. "After all, one can never be sure quite how your sort will behave."

"My sort, eh?" said Urgum. His voice was calm and reasonable. "I'll tell you how my sort behave. You approach me with a bit of respect, I appreciate that,

and we all pass by happily. But if you think you'll impress me by trying to look tough, I'll have to educate you."

"Don't be a fool." Gastan snorted. "Don't you realize I've got six armed men?"

"Six, is it?" muttered the savage, looking blankly at the slaves. "And what does that mean exactly?"

"It means there's six of them and one of you!" replied Gastan haughtily.

"Nope, now you've lost me." Urgum reached

towards the leather holster strapped around his horse. "Six, one – they're just number words aren't they? Never had much use for numbers myself. You can't eat them, you can't fight with them, in fact I can't see the point in numbers at all. No, this is more my sort of thing..."

Urgum slid his massive axe out of the holster, and then gave his horse a slap to send it out of the way. For once, the beast obeyed him and ambled off without complaint because it knew things were about to get seriously messy. The slaves hastily lowered the sedan sofa to the ground and formed a human shield facing Urgum.

"Father," said Divina calmly. "This is a pointless waste of good slaves. He is going to kill them all unless you tell them to put their swords away. Oh, and then he's going to kill us."

For the first time Urgum looked properly at the girl sitting beside the older man. She sat tall, her black hair was piled high on her head and set with silver combs, and the deep blue robe on her elegant shoulders made her look ... well, she looked rather smart. Urgum had never had much time for girls because they moaned about getting scars and smelt strange and if you picked a fight with a girl your mates would all laugh and call you soft. But this one had caught his attention. Her skin was light-tanned and she wasn't too thin like most softhand women thought it was so clever to be, but the really telling point about her was her hands. They were gently clasped and lay relaxed in her lap in contrast to her father's fingers which were drumming nervously on the arm of the sedan.

"He can't kill them *all*!" retorted her father.

Divina looked at Urgum curiously through half-closed eyes, as if she was trying to tell what he was thinking. To his surprise, her gaze made him feel rather awkward, so he raised his axe to his shoulder and did a big snarl to make himself feel better.

"Oh yes, he can kill them all," she announced at last with the faintest of smiles. "Well you can, can't you?"

Urgum's mouth was so dry that he was unable to speak, so he just nodded. In fact, he was so pleased that this softhand girl had recognized his talent that he kept nodding and nodding and nodding and only realized that he was looking extremely silly and ought to stop nodding when she raised her left eyebrow. In that one small facial movement she had said, "Yes, you are a powerful savage and we're all about to face a really horrible death, but frankly it wouldn't impress me much. Isn't there anything you can do better than that?"

Urgum looked at the slaves in front of him. They were all about his age and height, and from the way they held their swords he could see that two of them had had a bit of basic gladiatorial training, but the rest were just hoping to get a lucky strike in. They were strong, too, but years of heaving round sedan sofas had developed all the wrong muscles and consequently they were built for steady burden not fast combat. They were also scared, but they had every right to be. Just the smell of the blood-crazed adrenaline that came off Urgum was enough to terrify novices. Urgum wasn't by nature the merciful type, but these lads didn't deserve to die. Besides, he sensed that killing them wouldn't be enough to impress this girl, and after the way she'd raised that scornful eyebrow at him, he wanted to impress her more than anything. But if killing everybody wasn't going to work, what could he do?

The axe twitched in his hands. The slaves all bunched closer together and stuck their swords out further. It was pitiful. It would only take Urgum a few quick swipes to leave six severed arms lying in the sand still clutching their swords.

"Well?" snapped Gastan at the slaves. "What are you waiting for? Get him!"

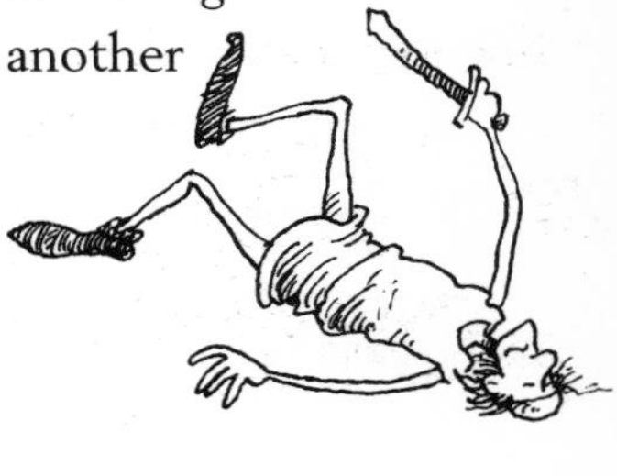

With a deft flick, Urgum tossed his axe up in the air so that it spun right over, then caught the heavy metal head in his hands, leaving the blunt handle sticking out towards the slaves. To his delight, the girl gasped in surprise and her eyes opened as wide as ostrich eggs. Absolutely beautiful huge deep dark brown eyes she had, she was seriously worth staring at, and was there even just another hint of a smile aimed at him? *Oh please, let her smile at me,* thought Urgum as he smashed the end of the axe handle into the nearest slave's teeth.

A plain staff or even a spear handle would have been a better weapon. It would have been longer, lighter and above all Urgum wouldn't have had the weight of the lethal axe head at the wrong end to cope with. A couple of the slaves were tougher than he'd thought. Still, within a few heartbeats he had shoved the end of the axe handle through a second set of teeth, broken two wrists, snapped one forearm and two ankles, and he had ripped an ear off and tossed it at the old man.

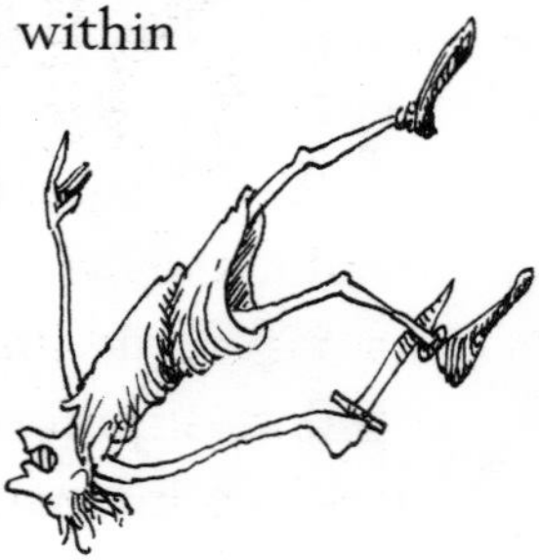

Urgum stood back and took a breath, thinking that would be enough to impress without showing off, but to his frustration there were still a couple of slaves feebly attempting to prod their swords in his direction.

"Sorry lads," he said. "I thought I'd finished. Come on then, I'll ditch the axe and you can give it your best shot."

Urgum tossed his axe aside, deliberately turning

away from the remaining slaves. Just as he expected, he heard the sharp draw of breath as they both lunged towards his back. He sidestepped neatly, avoiding the two sword-points, and then with a massive double-handed punch he smacked one slave's head straight into the other with a satisfying

SKLONCH.

He stepped over the fallen bodies and then straightened himself up to face the girl. He was rather proud of himself and why shouldn't he be? He'd just taken out six sword-wielding slaves with nothing more than an axe handle, and what's more, none of them had been damaged permanently. They could all be patched up and saved, so it hadn't been a waste of good slaves after all. She must be pleased, not to mention impressed, so was she going to smile?

"All right, savage, you've proved your point!" snapped her father. "Now go."

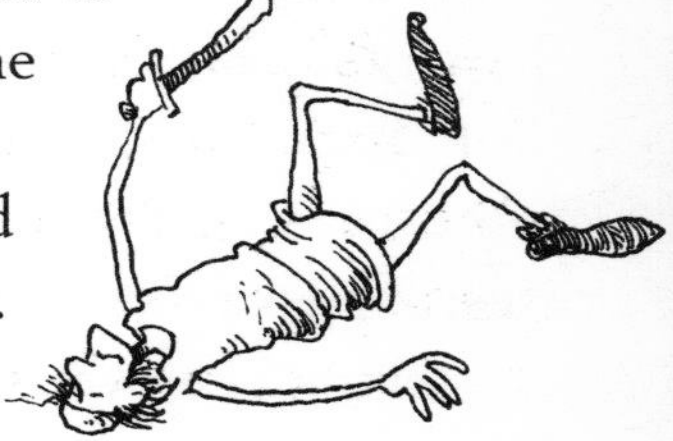

"It's not for you to give the orders, Father." The girl looked Urgum straight in the eye. "It's for him."

Urgum liked that answer. It's what he would have said himself if he'd thought of it in time. And although she hadn't smiled yet, he could see the girl's eyes were flickering over him. Surely she liked what she saw? *Once she's done the visual tour she'll be smiling,* thought Urgum. He'd just have to wait a moment, and in the meantime all he could do was stand there, holding his breath, trying not to tremble. But the girl's gaze seemed to have got stuck on his left thigh. Urgum looked down and saw a thick stream of blood coming from a fresh gash in his trousers. One of the slaves must have got lucky with his sword. He stuck his finger inside to check how deep the wound was and his nail scragged a raw nerve.

"Ow!" He winced without thinking, then glanced back at the girl.

"Wimp," she said, and sniffed.

Urgum was furious, partly with the girl but mainly with himself. He should have just taken the lot out with his axe. But what would the point of that have been? He knew that even if he chopped the girl to bits, somehow she would still be staring at him and he would still be holding his breath as he waited to see whether she was going to smile or raise her eyebrow.

All that had happened over twenty summers ago, but the memory was as fresh to Urgum as yesterday. Now he found himself standing in the mouthway of the cragg and, once again, he was staring at the same girl and holding his breath. Admittedly, she'd put on a bit of weight (but not nearly as much as Urgum), a few grey flecks had appeared in that rich mountain of hair, and the joys of raising seven barbaric sons in a cave had added a few gentle lines around her eyes, but it was the same girl. And once again Urgum was holding his breath as he waited to see whether she was going to smile or raise that eyebrow.

The Time Shift

The signs weren't good.

"How's my likkoo pwetty thuggar lipth been then?" Urgum asked, trying to be jolly.

But Divina's mouth didn't look like it had likkoo pwetty thuggar lipth. It looked like it was ready to bite his head off and spit his eyes out.

"We've had quite a trip," he added, as if he thought she was really interested. "We've been right around the far side of the Forgotten Crater. But don't you worry, you weren't forgotten! Look."

Urgum held out the bag of jewels, which she ignored.

"How kind of you to remember to come home," said Divina.

Urgum laughed loudly, pretending that she'd meant it as a joke. "Ho ho ho." He slapped his leg. "Of course we remembered to come home! After all, we've only been gone for the afternoon. Well, admittedly, it got a bit dark so we stayed over the night. And the next night. And the next, but it hasn't been that long. The crater only froze over the once, so be reasonable, it's not like it's been a whole year or anything. Well not quite. Has it? Anyway, tell me honestly, did you change the password?"

"Yes."

"Oh! Right, well what a good idea. In fact Olk and me have been having a bit of a laugh about it actually. So ... um ... when did you change it?"

"About ten years ago."

"TEN?" The seven sons gasped. They were completely mystified. It hadn't seemed at all like ten years. Only Urgum seemed unconcerned.

"Ten years, eh?" said Urgum. "Oh well, that's not so bad. Ten is the next number after one. Isn't it?"

"NO!" snapped Divina.

"It's two after one, Dad," said Ruinn. "Then it's three, then four, five, six, seven, eight, nine and THEN ten."

"Well you might have told me before!" said Urgum. "No wonder we're so late." He turned back to Divina. "I'm so sorry, I had no idea. I blame all this fancy mathematics. But surely it can't have been all those years?"

Divina scowled. "Oh yes it was, and I can prove it!"

"You're trying to frighten me, aren't you? Well you can't!" said Urgum.

"Oh yes I can!"

"Impossible! I'm Urgum the Axeman. How can you

scare me? Come on, let's see your worst!"

"You asked for it." Divina turned to call into the cave: "Molly!"

Immediately something shot out from the cave entrance. With a shriek of delight and a scampering of feet it flew across the basin, ducked past Olk, and threw itself around Urgum's neck.

"Dad!" it cried.

The Divine Joke

Urgum's eyes almost popped from his head. Very carefully, he unwound two slim arms from his neck and lowered them towards the ground. He took a step back, blinked, wiped his eyes, shook his head and blinked again, but still the thing in front of him wouldn't disappear.

"It's a girl!" shouted the seven sons.

"She called him DAD!" Ruff hooted.

Ruinn snorted. "Urgum is the father of a little GIRL!"

"A girlie girl..."

"...dresses..."

"...flowers..."

"...skipping..."

"AAARGHHHHH!"

Urgum screamed for so loud and so long that no one noticed the rumbling noises from far up and away...

* * *

The twin gods were thundering with laughter.

"So, be honest." Tangal wiped the tears of mirth from her eyes. "What do you think?"

"Fabulous!" admitted Tangor, who was still fighting off a final fit of the giggles. "Although I can't see why you added the ten years until the girl showed up. It's sheer genius, but do you really think she can change his ways?"

"Of course she can," said Tangal. "Up until now Urgum has only ever had to live for himself. He knew that if anything happened to him, Divina and the boys would all be quite capable of surviving without him. But now there's a little girl, things are suddenly very different."

"You mean ... you mean..." Tangor was starting to shake again so much that he could hardly get the words out. "You mean Urgum will have to show some ... *responsibility*?"

Beneath them, the clouds boomed and rocked as the gods guffawed mightily.

"He's got no choice," Tangal said, when she'd recovered her breath. "If he let anything happen to his little daughter, he'd curl up and die of shame."

"Then bang goes his chance of eternally stuffing his face at our dining table," said Tangor. "Hah! He'd be lucky if we gave him so much as a packet of crisps and a divine yoghurt."

"Good, isn't it?" said Tangal. "Now he'll have to settle down. There will be no more dashing around stupidly risking his life any more."

"And no more sudden panics for us!" said Tangor.

"It's a funny thing." Tangal sighed contentedly. "Urgum has always faced up to giant bulls, deadly snakes and enemy gangs armed with swords, arrows and cannons and none of them could stop him doing whatever he liked. But faced with a ten-year-old girl, poor Urgum won't have a chance."

While the thunder died away, Urgum had quite sensibly fainted and the sons gathered round his collapsed body.

"The shock's killed him!" Robbin gasped.

"Great!" said Rakk. "I'll have his boots."

"Why you?" demanded Rekk. "They fit me better."

"Oi!" said Molly. "You get off him."

"Oh?" said Rekk and Rakk. "And what's it got to do with you?"

"This is my father and he's going to be all right. After all, he is Urgum the Axeman, isn't he?"

On hearing his name Urgum's eyes opened.

To his horror, the girl was still there.

"Well?" said Molly. "You are Urgum the Axeman, aren't you?"

"Er ... am I?" Urgum sat up cautiously.

"The savagest slaughterer, the roughest rider, the dirtiest fighter and the foulest-ever-smelling living legend of barbarian folklore?"

Urgum nodded. "I do my best."

"Mum's told me all about you, Dad."

Dad! The very word made Urgum wince and grit his teeth. The girl was leaping around him happily.

"Oh Dad Daddy Dad Dad!" chanted Molly. "After all this time it's so nice to have someone I can call Dad, Dad."

"Divina!" Urgum begged. "Can we talk about this? It's a joke isn't it? You've just borrowed her? Or did you carve her out of your mother?"

"No joke, Urgum," said Divina. "Molly is yours."

"But how can that be? Little girls don't just turn up on their own."

Divina stared back at him, stony-faced. She was well aware that something very peculiar was going on, because when her sons had set off on the trip, they had been a rough teenage rabble, and yet here they were back after ten years, still looking like the same rough teenage rabble. It was as if those ten years had never passed, and yet in that time she had raised a ten-year-old daughter. Obviously the facts didn't fit together but silly little things like that didn't matter to Divina.

But there was one fact that *did* matter to Divina and it was this: whatever she said was right, and if Urgum disagreed then he was wrong. This fact had always kept her going and helped her to deal with all the curious and unexplainable events that happened in the Lost Desert. So, taking a deep breath and keeping this in mind, Divina presented her theory on how Molly came to be.

"The night before you set off," she said, tapping her foot on the ground impatiently, "remember bed time? After you blew out the candle? Before you rolled over and went to sleep? Do you remember anything else happening?"

"Er ... no!" Urgum blushed furiously.

"Oh yes he does!" The boys cheered. "Wahey! What happened, Dad?"

"Shhh!" Urgum pleaded with Divina. He hated this kind of conversation. "But surely we didn't..."

It was no use. The eyebrow was raised and so, as

usual, Divina was right and he was wrong.

"And that's why this is your daughter," said Divina, "and you don't come home until you admit it. OLK!"

The giant sentry staggered to his feet.

"You heard what I said, Olk. They don't come in until Molly says so."

Divina swept back in through the cragg entrance, marched across the basin and disappeared into their cave.

"So how about it, Dad?" said Molly, tugging Urgum's battle apron. "I've been dead looking forward to you coming back. You're going to teach me everything about being a barbarian and make me as fearless and savage as you."

"Look here, little girl," said Urgum. "I don't know who you are or what your game is, but it's not funny."

The seven sons laughed. "Yes it is!"

"Oh, I understand," said Molly, trying not to be upset. "Mum explained that you might be a bit shocked to see me. So look, I've got you a present to make you feel better."

"A present?" asked Urgum. He wasn't used to presents. Usually, if he wanted anything he just took it. Astonished, he allowed Molly to grab his hand and slip something inside it. When he opened his fingers he was

horrified to find himself holding a little chain of flowers.

"It's a necklace," said Molly proudly. "I grew all the flowers myself in my flower bed."

"Put it on then, Daddy," said Ruff. "Let's see the tough barbarian with his little pretty flower necklace!"

"That must be my brother Ruff, I suppose," said Molly giving him an unimpressed look. For a moment Ruff was surprised at being identified but then he just looked smug instead.

"Of course," he said. "Mum will have told you all about me."

"Not much," said Molly. "Just that you were the stupid one."

"Oi, little girl!" shouted Ruff. "Did you just call me stupid?"

"Yes, because you think my dad's too scared to put on a necklace."

"Well he is scared!" declared Ruff. Behind him the boys all grinned, but their faces froze as Urgum turned on them, his axe already in his hand.

"My dad isn't scared of anything," said Molly. "Are you, Dad?"

"Dead right I'm not scared." Urgum growled at the boys. "You lot better listen to this little girl. I'm Urgum the Axeman and I'm scared of nothing!"

"Go on then, Dad." Molly nudged him.

"Go on what?"

"Show them you're not scared," she said. "Put your necklace on."

Urgum was completely gobsmacked. All his instincts told him to rip up the flower necklace and throw the girl into the tar hole, but his imagination was playing strange tricks on him. It was as if there were tiny voices whispering in his ears:

"Urgum, that's the easy way out!"

"Do you want to be remembered as the savage who was scared of a few flowers?"

It didn't make sense! Had he panicked when the Giant Eagle of Gomah had snatched him up in her claws? No! Had he wet his boots when cornered by Taurassic the six-headed bull? No! So why did this little flower necklace make his hand tremble so much? Urgum looked down at the little girl who was so proud to be standing at his side, defending his honour. He looked across at his supposedly marvellous sons as they all jeered at him. For the first time, he realized that natural savagery might not be the right option. Putting on that necklace would take a strange kind of bravery he'd never attempted before. It was the ultimate test in courage and he knew he must not fail.

Facing his sons and holding his axe high ready to strike at the slightest smirk, Urgum put the necklace over his head. The seven sons clamped their lips tight shut and barely dared to breathe. They knew it would only take the smallest snigger for that axehead to fly among them taking chunks of twitching flesh with it.

"Wow, Dad!" Molly gasped in admiration. "You've scared them silly! Mum told me you were tough, but I never thought you'd be so cool with it."

"Cool?" said Urgum delightedly, but trying to sound cool to fit with his new image.

"The only thing she didn't tell me was how handsome you were," said Molly.

"Didn't she?" Urgum immediately forgot his new image and, tossing his axe to the ground, he did a completely uncool little skip of delight.

"No, but that'll be because you're so ugly," said Molly. "But I still love you, Dad."

And with that she reached up, threw her arms around Urgum's neck and gave him a big kiss. The sons could hold it back no longer.

"Oi, you with the flowers on..." cried Rekk.

"...give us a kiss too, Daddy!" shouted Rakk.

All the boys were in hysterics apart from Ruff, who was rather excited. He realized that this was a chance to get his own back on the girl for calling him stupid – and nobody would dare argue with him.

"You're being laughed at, Father," he said in his most pompous voice.

"Too right he is!" Ruinn hooted. "Ha ha ha!"

"It won't do," said Ruff. "You're supposed to be a true barbarian, Dad. To avenge this mockery, blood must be spilt."

"What do you mean, blood?" asked Urgum.

"The girl!" Ruff pointed at Molly. "She's the one who brought this upon you. You know what you have to do. Blood, blood blood..."

The other boys joined in the chant excitedly.

"...blood, blood, blood..."

Ruff strode over and picked Urgum's great axe up off the ground. Then, very solemnly, he put it into Urgum's massive hands.

"But ... what would your mother say?" asked Urgum.

"Mother isn't a true barbarian," replied Ruff smugly.

"But you are, and you've been laughed at. So do it, Urgum."

Urgum was trapped. Every decision he'd ever made had always been simple because being a barbarian meant you were always right – but he'd never had to face a test like this before. If he failed now, his entire barbarian reputation would become worthless. He might as well become a crop picker or a soap merchant: he might as well die. Slowly he raised his axe over his head. Molly stood in front of him with a curious expression on her face.

"Run!" he hissed. "Go on, run away. Quick."

"Why should I?" asked Molly. "I want to be a brave barbarian like you."

Urgum's axe had never felt so heavy in his hands. "Aren't you scared?"

"Of course not," replied Molly. "Barbarians aren't scared. Besides, my dad isn't going to kill me."

She stared straight at Ruff who was standing next to Urgum, looking extremely proud of himself. "And do you know why my dad isn't going to kill me?" asked Molly.

"Why?" said Ruff.

"Because he's a great big fat old softie!" Molly

jumped up and wiggled her fingers into both of Urgum's armpits at once.

With a helpless roar of mirth he dropped the axe. "Gerroff, no, stoppit, that's unfair, mercy, I give in, HELP!"

As Urgum sank to his knees, Molly thrust her fingers one final time into his armpits and then stood back.

"Had enough yet?" she asked.

"Stoppit," pleaded Urgum between gulps of laughter. Tears poured from his eyes. "That's it. Quits. No more tickling and I won't hack you to bits."

"Promise?" asked Molly.

"Promise," Urgum gasped, trying to catch his breath.

Behind him, the other sons watched in amazement.

"Hey!" said Ruinn. "What about the blood? The mockery needs to be avenged and all that, or doesn't being a true barbarian matter to you any more?"

But there was blood and quite a lot of it. When Urgum's axe fell, it sliced into Ruff's leg. Now, the number one son was lying on the ground whimpering and moaning as a large red pool spread out around him.

"Does that hurt?" asked Robbin.

Ruff could only squeak in agony.

"Then that's good enough for me." Robbin smiled at

Molly and, stepping forward, he reached out to shake her hand. "Well done, little girl. I'm Robbin."

"I know," said Molly. "Mum said you were the nice one."

"Aw!" Robbin blushed slightly. "So, have you worked out who the others are?"

"Easy," said Molly. "Rekk and Rakk are always starting fights with each other."

"It's not me that starts it!" shouted Rekk and Rakk together. Pointing at each other, they continued: "It's him! You liar." "Did you call me a liar? I'll kick you for that..."

Then the twins tried to kick each other at the same time and fell over.

"Raymond is the one with the brain," said Molly.

"That's fair enough." Ruinn pulled Raymond's brain from

one of the bags. "Look, it's got these brilliant little purple bits that bulge when he's thinking."

"And you must be Ruinn," said Molly. "The weird one. See, I know all six of you."

"But there's seven of us," said Robbin.

"Oh ... oh yes," said Molly, counting the boys. "Mum forgot to mention the Other One."

By now Urgum had got to his feet.

"Boys ... and wimps." He looked down at Ruff. "I don't know how it's come about, but we've been blessed. You've got a new sister, and I've got my very own daughter."

There was a muttering of agreement and a nodding of heads. Molly beamed with pride.

"Hooray!" she cheered, skipping around Urgum and tossing flower petals at the boys. "I'm going to be a barbarian!"

"HOLD IT!"

snarled Urgum.

Molly stopped in her tracks. "What?"

"You might be my daughter, but NO WAY will you ever be a barbarian," said Urgum.

"And why not?"

"Because..." Urgum waved an important finger in the air while he thought of a few reasons, "...because ONE, you're a girl and TWO, you're skipping and throwing flower petals and THREE, you haven't got any scars and FIVE, barbarians don't win gruesome combats to the death by tickling people..."

"You missed out four," said Molly.

"...and most of all, FOUR, you can't be a barbarian because you can do stupid numbers in the right order," snapped Urgum.

"We can all do numbers except you," Ruinn wanted to say but he didn't.

The boys all knew that when Urgum was on the subject of what it took to be a barbarian, it was highly dangerous to answer him back. It certainly took more nerve than they had. But it didn't take more nerve than Molly had.

"Oh really?" She took a deep breath. "Well maybe if you'd been at home bringing me up properly rather than leaving Mum to cope while you went dandying around pretending to chase unicorns I WOULD be a barbarian, and just because I've spent ten years planting flowers and learning to write and do my numbers it doesn't mean it's too late for me to be a barbarian PROVIDING you start making a proper effort and you're not too fat or lazy or cowardly to do anything about it."

There was a strange noise as all seven boys gulped nervously. Dandying? Surely she hadn't accused Urgum the Axeman of dandying?

Even though they didn't know exactly what dandying was, they knew exactly what it wasn't. It wasn't the sort of thing that you accused the fiercest savage of the Lost Desert of doing. Oh dear, this was seriously bad.

Slowly, they all backed away from the barbarian and the little girl. Over their years with Urgum they had grown used to seeing him perform the most gruesome and grisly deeds, but none of them felt prepared for what they were surely about to witness.

Urgum looked like he had been hit on the forehead with the mallet that Olk used to stun hippopotamuses. NOBODY ever spoke to him like that. He stood there, completely transfixed with rage, his mind knotting itself up as he tried to decide how best to teach this ghastly female girl thing the lesson of her life. Should he chuck her in the bear pit? String her up over a boiling geyser? Cover her in honey and let the termites burrow into her skin? Dangle her over a grid of red-hot iron spikes? All of them at once? Who did she think she was, standing in front of him in her little girl dress with her thin arms folded and looking utterly unimpressed? He'd make her regret the day she presumed to lecture the fiercest savage that the Lost Desert had ever known. Oh yes indeed, she'd be so sorry and so begging for forgiveness and he'd be so right and she'd be so wrong that she would never ever ever speak to him like that ever again ever.

But then the very worst thing that could have possibly happened happened. Molly raised her left eyebrow.

Urgum gasped in horror. The girl knew exactly what he was planning and she simply didn't care. She was no more impressed with him than her mother had been all those years ago. Every muscle in his body surrendered and went completely floppy. His jaw dropped open, his tongue hung out and he started to sway. Robbin and Ruinn quickly ran back and held his arms to steady him.

"There," said Molly. "I've been waiting a long time to say what I just said and now I've said it, that's it said so we'll say no more about it. So when you've all quite finished gawping at me, are you coming inside to the cave or what?"

Urgum blinked and shook himself free. Robbin and Ruinn went to grab Ruff and haul him to his feet while the others collected the horses. Molly skipped past Olk, but as Urgum and the seven sons approached...

"PASSWORD!"

boomed Olk.

"Molly, wait right there!" ordered Urgum, trying to cling on to a final shred of dignity. "We still don't know the new password!"

"That's all right," said Molly coming back. "Olk knows it, so why don't you ask him?"

"That's not how the system works!" said Urgum.

"Honestly!" said Molly. "Use your brains a bit. Olk, do you know the new password?"

"Password." Olk nodded.

"Then what is it?"

"HONEYSUCKLE."

"HONEYSUCKLE?"

Urgum and the seven sons gasped.

"Enter," said Olk.

"See?" said Molly. "I told you he knew it. Thanks Olk."

Urgum and his sons looked at each other, astonished.

"Well?" demanded Molly. "Say 'Thank you. Olk' and come in. "

And so, very cautiously, Urgum and the seven sons said "Thank you, Olk," stepped under the nasty blade and went in.

GOLGARTH CRAGG
PART TWO
WHEN THINGS CHANGED

The Ugly Friend

"Who's been a naughty boy then?" A deep voice rang out across Golgarth basin as Urgum and the sons followed Molly towards their cave.

"Mungoid!" Urgum dashed over to where his oldest, ugliest and bestest friend was sitting on his steps. Mungoid the Ungoid had been carving himself a set of new battle teeth out of some rhino horns. He slipped them into his mouth.

"Whash do you shink of theesh teesh?" he said, gnashing away.

But Urgum had no time for teeth. "Mungoid, my mate of old. Tell me honestly. What exactly has been going on?"

"Thinsh have chanshed," said Mungoid. "For one thinth I've goth thum new teesh."

"So? I've got some new teeth too," said Urgum.

"Have you?" Mungoid took his teeth out. He was slightly jealous.

"Yes, and that's not all. I've got a new mouth, a new head, and a whole new body with legs and arms and everything!"

"Really?" Mungoid looked Urgum up and down doubtfully. He still looked like the same filthy old savage he'd always known.

"I've got a NEW DAUGHTER!" bleated Urgum.

"Oh, you mean Molly," said Mungoid. "She's a great kid. She helps me with plucking the ostriches. She pulls the feathers out while I hold them still."

"Don't you kill them first?"

"Nah. Where's the fun in that?"

"Fair enough," agreed Urgum. "But where did the Molly girl come from?"

Mungoid raised a massive eyebrow. "The usual place. She was born the winter after you set off on the Unicorn Hunt."

"Are you having a joke?" demanded Urgum. "She should only be a baby."

"Things have changed in ten years," said Mungoid. He held up his fingers to show Urgum how many winters this was.

Urgum shook his head in disbelief. "No way was that ten years! Do I look like I've been hunting for ten winters?"

"Hard to say," said Mungoid.

"All right then, I'll make it easier. Do I *stink* like I've been unicorn hunting for ten winters? Go on, have a sniff."

Mungoid sniffed Urgum.

"Hmmm," said Mungoid. "Well you smell pretty bad, but I wouldn't say that's ten years' worth. Unless of course you've had a wash..."

Mungoid thought this was so funny that he took a deep breath so he could do a big booming laugh. But then he remembered that the merest suggestion of a wash to Urgum was a gross insult punishable by utter death, so he clamped his hand over his mouth to stop the laugh coming out.

Unfortunately the laugh was already on its way and, finding Mungoid's mouth blocked, it changed direction and shot out of his nose making a noise like a squashed duck.

Urgum glowered at him suspiciously. "Did you say I'd had a wash?"

"Well, things have changed," said Mungoid. "You might have done."

"Some things do NOT change! And will you stop saying 'things have changed'?"

"I'll try," said Mungoid. "But it isn't easy."

"Why?" asked Urgum.

"Because things have changed."

"ENOUGH!" Urgum pointed a threatening finger at Mungoid. "I'm warning you, will you stop saying ... what's that smell?"

"I never said, 'What's that smell?'" said Mungoid.

"But what IS that smell?" Urgum sniffed the air excitedly. His threatening finger was still pointing at Mungoid, but when it realized that the rest of Urgum wasn't being threatening any more, the finger felt a bit silly trying to look threatening all by itself. So instead it decided to do a funny little wiggle and fold itself away.

"Most of the smell is you," said Mungoid.

"No, the other smell," said Urgum who was starting to dribble. "It's ... er, nice!"

"Oh *that* smell," said Mungoid. "That's coming from your place. Molly got bored with eating burnt animals for tea every night so she's been helping Divina invent some new recipes."

"Wow!" exclaimed Urgum. "I didn't know food could smell like that!"

"Ah," said Mungoid. "But things have changed."

"STOP SAYING THAT!"

In a fury Urgum reached for his axe, so Mungoid put in his new battle teeth.

"I'll axe you to pieces!" shouted Urgum.

"Noth if I bith your armsh off you won'th," gnashed Mungoid.

"This is great!" Urgum swung his axe narrowly missing Mungoid's neck. "We haven't had a good fight for years, have we?"

CHOMP!

Mungoid's teeth sank into Urgum's arm, but when Urgum pulled away the teeth plopped out of Mungoid's mouth.

"They've locked on to my arm," said Urgum.

"Bah!" said Mungoid. "I'll need to get some big screws and fix them into my jaws properly."

"How do I get them off?" asked Urgum, wrestling with the teeth.

"You need a bit of twisted metal like a broken spoon or something," said Mungoid.

"Oh never mind. My arm isn't going blue or anything so I'll get them off later. When's the last time you had a good fight anyway?"

"Ages ago," admitted Mungoid. "Remember, just before you set off we were raided by the Fat Mutts of Nugg?"

"The Mutts of Nugg!" Urgum smiled. "We covered over the bear pit with a net and they all fell right in it!"

"That's it," said Mungoid. "And the ones that the bear didn't eat, we hung them up by the neck."

By now they were both laughing.

"All of them at once..."

"...and all from the same branch..."

"...of the Lynching Tree..."

"...and they were so heavy..."

"...the tree fell over!"

Ha ha ha ha.

"Poor old Lynching Tree," said Urgum sadly. "We had some fun there as kids, didn't we Mungoid? I remember as a little savage the bodies would be hanging up there twitching and we'd be underneath lighting little fires and getting the last few screams out of them. Yes, things just won't be the same without that old tree."

"Look," said Mungoid pointing over to a tall tree in the hottest corner of the rock basin. Urgum blinked in disbelief.

"But we chopped it up to burn the Fat Mutts!"

"Then we planted a new tree," said Mungoid.

"But it was only a stick plant when I left," said Urgum.

"Look at it now," said Mungoid. "That's how long you've been away. Believe me, things have changed."

"STOP SAYING THAT!"

"Might stop, might not."

"But you always used to do what I said," complained Urgum.

"Ahh." Mungoid nodded wisely. "But things have changed."

An Uncomfortable Party

If Urgum was feeling shocked and confused, he might have been consoled by the fact that Divina was feeling almost as uncomfortable as he was. She was in the kitchen of their cave, supervising the cooking of a grand dinner that she had been carefully planning for months, and the unexpected return of Urgum and the seven sons had rather upset her guest list. But this was the least of her problems.

When Urgum had set off on the Unicorn Hunt, their cave hadn't had this rather fine kitchen. It hadn't even had a rough kitchen or any other sort of kitchen or anything else for that matter. The last time Urgum saw it, the cave had just been a deep dark hole in the rock. This suited Urgum fine because, being a true barbarian, he didn't approve of modern luxuries such as hygiene, warmth and privacy. He wanted his boys to live the hard way of the savage, and not to be tempted by the cosy habits of the softhands, so it was a god's guess how Urgum would react when he saw what Divina described as "home improvements". She knew he'd never harm her, but maybe he'd just disappear back into the desert and never return. Even though she was furious with him for being gone ten years, underneath it all, she was glad to see him back and always would be.

That's why, when Molly had brought everyone in past Olk, Divina was hugely relieved when Urgum went off to speak to Mungoid rather than coming straight over to the cave with the boys. It meant that they would see the changes before he did and so they could make their own minds up without having to agree with him. Thankfully, they were delighted to find that they now had their own big bedroom with a door and wouldn't have to sleep with one eye always open looking for night predators slithering in towards them.

Her biggest son, Robbin, had taken a special interest

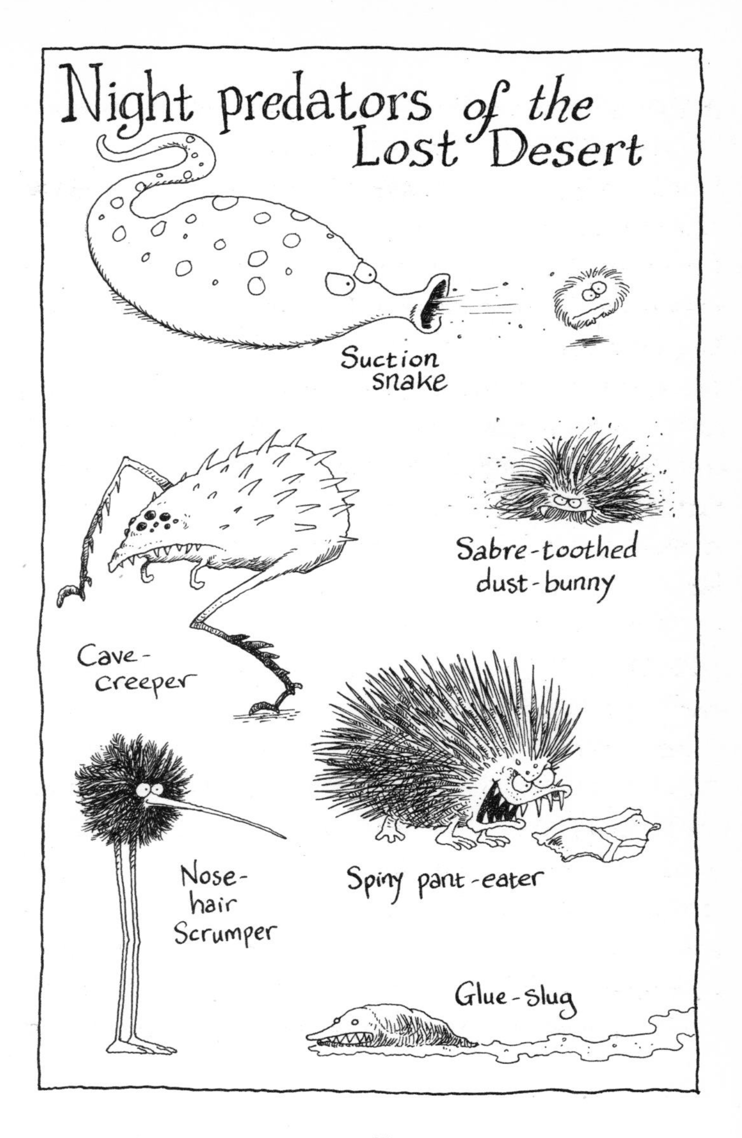
Night predators of the Lost Desert
Suction snake
Sabre-toothed dust-bunny
Cave-creeper
Nose-hair Scrumper
Spiny pant-eater
Glue-slug

in the kitchen and, while the others were happily fighting over who slept where, he'd come to learn about making gravy. So why had Divina risked upsetting Urgum by changing the cave?

Up until recently Divina had fitted in with Urgum's lifestyle with minimal complaint. After all, it had been her choice to abandon the lazy softhand life to marry him and she was so proud to be the wife of the fiercest barbarian that the Lost Desert had ever known that she hadn't wanted to dint his reputation by doing anything silly like putting up curtains or cooking broccoli. To her surprise, the odd mixture of savages living at Golgarth Cragg had immediately made her so welcome that she was embarrassed, especially when she compared this to how softhands treated outsiders. To a softhand, being different in any way meant you were inferior, and therefore to be ignored, insulted or exploited. But to a savage, if you were different it meant you were useful. (Savages always appreciated any new skill or talent that you could share with the group, or at the worst you would be food, so either way, they were glad to see you.) Urgum, Olk and Mungoid were all different breeds of savage, but in the hard, wasted fringes of the desert, they knew they needed to respect and support each other to survive. Along with a few others they had made Golgarth Cragg their home and Divina felt very honoured to have been invited to join them. In many ways she found the savages were a lot more civilized than the softhands.

But in the time that Urgum had been away, two things had happened.

The first thing was that Molly had appeared and Divina felt that as much as it might suit seven boys to sleep on a cave floor open to sabre-toothed skunks and suction snakes, maybe it was unfair to expect a girl to do the same.

The second thing had been the casual utterance of one single unfortunate word.

On her visits to the market Divina often bumped into some of her old friends and even though they were always arrayed in the very latest fashions, riding plush sedan sofas, they never remarked that Divina was wearing home-made dresses and usually driving her own shopping chariot.

And even though they had money to spend whereas Divina only had animal skins and the occasional precious stone to trade, there was never any suggestion that she'd married beneath her, gone downhill or lost

touch with reality ... at least not to her face. That's because Divina was married to the fiercest savage that the Lost Desert had ever known and *nobody* said anything that might upset Divina to her face. Not only that, but Divina was the only person who had ever made Urgum have a wash and lived to talk about it. (This was such a nasty event that if anyone were to hear about it, they'd be sick.) So it was no wonder that everybody treated Divina with absolutely massive respect.

But even though her old friends always greeted her

with politeness and smiles, Divina had started to feel uncomfortable among them. Was it her imagination, or did their gentle laughter sometimes sound like a mean snigger behind her back? Were they really treating her as an equal? Then one hot morning, quite by chance, all Divina's suspicions were suddenly confirmed.

Molly was sitting out by the crossroads trying to sell a few little bracelets and chains that she'd made from her flowers. Divina was with her when the chancellor's wife Suprema passed and idly tossed a few small bronze tannas at Molly, then scooped up everything she'd made.

Molly was delighted and crawled around the ground picking the coins up.

"That was kind," Divina said.

"Oh honestly, Divina!" Suprema sneered. She had already squashed the flowers into a messy ball and dumped them down behind her. "Giving to beggars counts as charity, so I can just claim it back from the palace tax department."

Beggars? At that moment, Divina decided she would show her old friends that, although her lifestyle might be different, she was not by any means a beggar. Even though she'd got herself the toughest husband in the desert, she needed to show that it hadn't been at the expense of her domestic standards. She wanted to prove that just because a girl walks out on civilization, it doesn't mean civilization has to walk out on the girl.

That's why she had set her mind on giving a dinner party for some of the ladies of Laplace Palace. She realized it was going to take a massive amount of preparation – could she really invite her friends to leave their lavish homes to sit on the dirt floor of a draughty hole in the rock among the dead bats and lizards? No, she couldn't. Could she really expect them to hold sparkling conversations whilst eating burnt chunks picked from a large animal carcass? Again, no, she couldn't.

So she arranged for the cave to undergo a complete

transformation, and then she laboured away for days to prepare one of the finest meals the Lost Desert had ever seen. Once it was ready, all she had to do was casually invite the ladies in for a cosy meal and a chat and pretend that this is how she lived her life, and then the sniggering would stop.

But Divina hadn't reckoned on Urgum and the boys arriving home. Obviously they would hope to be fed too, and she had no doubts about what the ladies would think to their table manners, not to mention their belching competitions. What was even worse, her ladies were bound to arrive while she was gently breaking it to Urgum what she'd done to his beloved cave. It was going to take more than a stern look and an an eyebrow to control him then.

And that's why Divina was in her new kitchen making a massive dinner and feeling uncomfortable.

The New Neighbour

Meanwhile, out across the other side of Golgarth basin, Urgum was reaching for his axe to kill his best friend again when a tall red-haired woman in skirmish armour galloped in through the mouthway of the cragg. She carried a bow, and across her back hung a quiverful of arrows.

"Wow!" said Urgum excitedly. "It's a raid. Come on, let's get her!"

"No!" Mungoid hurriedly wiped his great nose on his sleeve and straightened his vest. "Calm down and watch. This is class."

As she leapt from her horse, the woman plucked a

slender arrow from the quiver and before her feet hit the ground she had already fired it.

TINK!

The arrow hit a rock and bounced back between the legs of a startled ostrich...

PONK!

The arrow ricocheted off a tortoise and shot directly between Urgum and Mungoid's open-mouthed faces...

CLANG!

It hit a small bell hanging outside a cave entrance along from Mungoid's...

Finally the arrow neatly dropped into a second quiver, hanging underneath the bell.

On hearing the sound, two meebobs hurried out towards the woman. They were small grey creatures with long beards, hair that reached the floor, short chunky hands and bare feet. Their huge eyes blinked uncomfortably in the daylight so, as quickly as they could, one took the reins of the archer's horse and the other caught the pair of spotted rabbits she tossed at him, then they scuttled back into the dark cave.

"And exactly who's that?" asked Urgum.

Beside him, Mungoid had licked his banana-sized fingers and was trying to smooth down the three hairs that stuck up from the top of his head. "Grizelda the Grisly," he replied in a hushed voice.

"Grizelda?" Urgum laughed. "That snotty little slave girl the Fat Mutts were dragging around? I thought you were going to eat her."

"SHHHH!" pleaded Mungoid. "She'll hear you!"

The tall red-haired woman didn't so much walk as

do a rhythmic glide in their direction. As she moved, her hair cascaded gently down her back like a succession of waves lapping on a beach. Mungoid scrambled to his feet and did a little bow.

"Good afternoon Grizelda," he said hopefully, as she passed by. In reward she turned her head slightly and although she didn't actually smile, she didn't not smile either. Mungoid sighed with joy and *twink plink dink,* his three hairs shot back up again.

"I'll be seeing you then!" he called as he turned to watch her flit up the steps to her own cave. Long after she'd disappeared inside Mungoid was still staring wistfully after her.

"Oooh," thought Urgum. "Things *have* changed!"

A Tale of Two Smells

Any sort of normal conversation with Mungoid had obviously come to an end, so Urgum decided it was time to get home and investigate what was smelling so interesting. He crossed the basin, then stepped out of the sunlight and into his friendly old cave. It was very dark, despite the best efforts of a flaming torch spluttering away on the wall. The smell was overpowering and Urgum's mouth was dribbling like a spring waterfall.

"What's that smell?" he called.

No answer. He peered into the gloom of the cave but it seemed to be empty. Urgum thought he might as

well start getting undressed. After all those months out hunting it was going to feel good to get his old leathers off and have a really deep satisfying scratch. He'd just pulled his trousers down when...

"Hi Dad!"

Urgum looked up and was amazed to see Molly had appeared at the darkest end of the cave. She was staring at him with a huge grin and eyes as wide as two full moons.

"Arghh!" He grabbed his axe. "Where did you come from?"

"I was in the kitchen," said Molly.

"The *what*?" asked Urgum. He'd never heard of a kitchen before and whatever a kitchen was, there definitely hadn't been one in his cave when he'd left.

"So what are you doing?" Molly giggled.

"I'm taking my trousers off." Urgum quickly pulled his trousers on again.

"MUM!" shouted Molly. "Come and look! Dad's taking his trousers off in the lounge!"

"In the *where*?" said Urgum.

"The lounge!"

"The lee-ow-un-je?"

And then, adding to Urgum's confusion, Divina stepped through the dark wall behind Molly.

"How do you two just walk through the wall like that?" he said.

"Don't change the subject," said Divina. "And from now on, I don't want any trousers off in the lounge."

"What's this lee-ow-un-je business?" shouted Urgum, waving his axe. "We are barbaric savages and we live in a CAVE and if I want to take my trousers off, then I will."

"Spoken like a true savage dad," said Molly. "That's so cool!"

"Don't encourage him, Molly!" Divina sniffed. "Being barbaric savages doesn't mean that we have to be unsophisticated. Look."

Divina pulled a pile of dried skins from a shelf. Urgum saw they were covered in scribbles and drawings which didn't mean a thing to him.

"What's that?" he asked.

"*Modern Savage* magazine," said Molly. "She's always reading it."

"It tells us how to improve our barbaric lifestyle," explained Divina.

"But it's great as it is!" said Urgum. "Why would we want to improve it?"

"For Molly," said Divina. "We've got a daughter now, and I want her to have all the things a young girl should have."

"Such as?"

"Well to start with," said Divina, "I want her to have a father who doesn't take his trousers off in the lounge."

"Pah!" Urgum snorted. "You can sit in your lee-ow-un-je and read your mag-uzz-een if you want to, but I'm not changing my lifestyle for anyone."

But just then Robbin, the largest son, walked through the wall behind Divina, carrying a fork.

"Oh no!" Urgum wailed. "Now even Robbin's at it! How do they do that?"

"Mum, the oil's boiling," said Robbin. "Is it time for the pepper juice?"

"Guess what we're making?" said Molly.

"Easy!" said Urgum, feeling reassured. At least he'd understood what Robbin was doing. "You're making someone talk. You've got them in boiling oil and you're about to squirt pepper juice in their eyes and then maybe scoop their brains out with that fork. See Divina? I told you we're barbaric savages."

"Er ... actually Dad, I'm helping to make your tea!" said Robbin. "What do you think of the smell?"

The smell! When Urgum had been getting undressed, his nose had wisely taken a rest so he'd forgotten about the smell. But now Urgum woke it up again and took a long deep *sniffffffffff* ... the smell was so utterly gorgeous that once Urgum had started his sniff, he couldn't stop and he started to swell up like a balloon.

"Of course he doesn't want any," said Divina to Robbin. "Because he doesn't like our new lifestyle."

"Don't be mean, Mum!" said Molly. "Hey Dad, do you want to see what we're making or not?"

Urgum nodded his head so hard that a shower of dribble flew everywhere. Finally he breathed out and nearly blew Molly over.

"Very well," said Divina. "If you behave yourself, we'll show you."

So Urgum put his axe down and did his best not to take his trousers off or shout or kill anybody for a while. Divina and Robbin went back down to the dark end of the cave and disappeared. Molly followed but

then, seeing Urgum hanging back uncertainly, she took his massive scabby old hand and pulled him towards the darkness. With his free hand he tugged the torch off the wall and advanced suspiciously. In the flickering light, he saw that three archways had been cut into the rock.

"Oh!" he said, sounding relieved. "So that's how you came through the wall. But how did these great big holes get here?"

"Mum's had a builder in," said Molly.

"A builder?" asked Urgum.

"While you were away having your fun, Mum's been here having hers." Molly giggled. "Come on, see what you think of the kitchen."

They stepped through the first archway and Urgum found himself in hungry barbarian heaven. In the middle of the vast cavern, a dead giraffe was hanging over a stack of burning logs. The beast had been impaled on a thick metal pole which was being slowly turned by a marvellous system of weights, pulleys and cogwheels. Thick woody smoke billowed up through a small hole in the roof and, as the sizzling juices dripped into the fire, flashes of flame spat out in all directions.

Robbin went to stir the contents of a little iron pot on a stove. "Better than torturing people, eh Dad?"

"Shlovva blobble dullup," said Urgum, unaware that his mouth was hanging wide open and his tongue was flapping about on his chest. Roast giraffe was his very absolute favouritest dinner. With tears of joy in his eyes he charged straight at the beast without a thought that the fire might burn his legs off.

KALANGGG!

Urgum's face smacked straight into a heavy metal plate that Robbin thrust in his way.

"Not yet, Dad," he said. "Wait until tea time."

"Whose side are you on?" pleaded Urgum, pointing at the giraffe.

"Molly's been showing me how to make sauce," said Robbin. "And it's not finished yet. So wait."

"Get out of my way! Or I'll take you apart, big boy!"

"Maybe." Robbin prodded him with the end of a spoon. "But if you do, you won't get any tea."

"Patience, Urgum!" said Divina, stepping between them. "Come on, you've got lots more to see first."

"More kitchens?" asked Urgum. "Yippee!"

Divina went back into the lounge and on through the second archway, followed by Urgum who was still clutching the torch.

"The boys' bedroom," announced Divina. "For our seven sons."

"Oh," said Urgum.

The room was almost as big as the lounge and lit with more burning torches around the walls. Several bearskins were laid out on the floor and naturally the boys were arguing over who had which. Ruinn was sitting on one skin and Raymond's bags were arranged on the one next to him.

"You better keep your side tidy Raymond," said Ruinn. "And no sleepwalking."

On another pair of skins, the twins Rekk and Rakk were fighting to be on the side nearest the door. Ruff was standing beside a skin with a big lump underneath it.

"Has anyone seen the Other One?" He sat down on the lump with a thump.

"Ooof!" said the lump.

"It's good to see them all settling in, isn't it?" said Divina, thinking Urgum was still behind her. When there was no answer she repeated the question: "I said it's good to see that..."

Just as Divina turned round to see an empty space where Urgum was supposed to be, she heard a

KADDONG

from the distant kitchen. She hurried back through to find Urgum with a saucepan wedged over his head and Molly swinging from the handle.

"I caught him trying to sneak up to the giraffe again, Mum," said Molly.

Together, Divina and Molly pulled on the saucepan handle and dragged Urgum back into the lounge. With an angry shake and a tug, Urgum ripped the pan off his head to see Divina standing in front of him, glaring, with her arms folded.

"Behave!" she warned him. "And before you eat, you have to look round the rest of the house and say how much you like it."

Urgum sulked mightily. “Why can’t I eat NOW?”

“Because it isn’t tea time,” said Divina.

“And besides,” added Molly, “it isn’t for you.”

“WHAT?”

“Oops!” said Molly. “I think I’ll leave you two to it.” And she dashed back into the kitchen.

“Why isn’t it for me?” demanded Urgum.

“I didn’t expect you back,” said Divina. “I’ve got some ladies coming.”

“Ladies? What ladies?”

“Some of my old friends from the palace,” said Divina. “I want Molly to learn how nice people behave. So you behave, too, or you won’t get anything at all.”

Urgum snarled. “Oh won’t I? Well in that case I think I’ll just get undressed in the lee-ow-un-je and go to sleep where I always sleep, in the middle of the floor. See what your nice ladies think to that.”

“You dare!” snapped Divina. “Because if you do, I’ll never make a smell like that in the kitchen again.”

Urgum fell silent.

“That’s better,” said Divina. “Now let me show you the rest of the house.”

“There’s more?” muttered Urgum. “How many builders have you had in here?”

"Just the one."

"One?" Urgum gasped, looking at the archways. "He must have had some amazing drills and hammers to do all this."

"No. Just a spoon."

"A SPOON? But it would have taken him years!"

"You've been away for ten years, remember!" Divina held up her fingers. "That's one, two, three, four..."

"All right all right!" said Urgum. "But how did you pay him? I hope you haven't been trading in softhand money, that stuff just attracts trouble."

"Don't get worked up. If you must know I was going to give him a few rubies from the jewel chest," said Divina. "But here comes the good news. He just disappeared one day, and never came back. I never gave him anything."

"Oh!" said Urgum. "Oh well, that's all right then."

Divina allowed herself a small sigh of relief, but it was only a very small one. She was still unsure how Urgum would react to the other structural and domestic changes that he hadn't seen yet. Maybe she'd leave it until later to show him...

"Are there any other structural and domestic changes that I haven't seen yet?" asked Urgum.

Divina took a deep breath, but the question was answered for her by some sniggering from the boys' room.

"What's up with you lot?" shouted Urgum.

Ruinn stuck his head out of the doorway. "Just wait till you see where you're sleeping!"

The boys all laughed. "Hah hah hah!"

Urgum turned on Divina. "What's all this?"

"You'll like it," said Divina. "At least, you will if you know what's good for you."

Holding his torch out in front of him, Urgum strode through the last archway to find himself in a small passage which had smaller archways leading off it. He looked through the first one to see a small cavelet with a thick bearskin laid out on a straw mattress, a neat arrangement of sacrificial knives on the wall and a pile of clothes in the corner. There was a bright pink fluffy rug on the floor.

"Arghh!" said Urgum.

"What's the matter, Dad?" asked Molly, coming in behind him.

"I can't sleep in here," said Urgum. "There's a pink fluffy rug on the floor!"

"Don't panic, Dad," said Molly. "This is my room."

"That's a relief!" Urgum sighed, with a relieved smile. "Can you imagine Urgum the Axeman sleeping in here? What would Mungoid say?"

"Here's where you sleep," said Molly, indicating the next archway.

Urgum stepped through and held up his flaming torch. Was it a trick of the light? Had he gone too long without sleep? Were the gods playing a mean joke on him?

* * *

Unknown to Urgum, up in the Halls of Sirrus, the barbarian twin gods were indeed enjoying themselves at his expense.

"What is he going to make of this?" Tangor roared with mirth.

Tangal chortled. "It'll give him something to think about, all right!"

Back in the bedroom, Urgum blinked desperately, but the vision in front of him would not go away. The walls and the entire ceiling of the bedroom were covered in cascades of shimmering silk, the floor was entirely quilted in a patchwork of tasselled cushions, a white marble table was overloaded with pots of make-up, dresses and shawls hung from wall hooks, and towering urns of flowers filled every corner. Worst of all, a large embroidered ragdoll with rosy cheeks and cherry lips smiled at him from the pillows of the four-poster bed.

Urgum tried to speak but so many rude words were coming out at once that they all got jammed together in his neck so no sound came out.

Divina sat on the bed and patted the cushion beside her.

"Speechless, eh?" She smiled, trying not to look

worried. "I don't blame you. It *is* nice isn't it? I've done it up just like the picture in *Modern Savage*. Now come and sit yourself down on our new bed, you tired old beast."

"What's that fat thing you're prodding?" asked Urgum.

"It's a nice big soft cushion," said Divina.

In a daze, with his mouth hanging open in disbelief, Urgum went to sit beside his wife. Slowly he lowered himself on to the cushion then jumped up again.

"IT HUGGED MY BOTTOM!" he exclaimed crossly. "I felt it. Urgh!"

"But it's lovely to sleep on," said Divina.

"I'M NOT SLEEPING ON THAT PILE OF SICK!" bellowed Urgum.

"Well, where are you going to sleep then?"

Urgum had spotted a final archway at the end of the passage. Waving his torch over his head he stomped angrily towards it.

"I'm sleeping in here!" he said, stepping inside.

"ARGHHHH!"

Divina and Molly looked through into the tiny cavelet to see the top half of Urgum sticking out of a hole in the floor.

"Just because you don't like cushions, that's no reason to throw yourself down the toilet," said Divina.

"The *what*?" Urgum tried to struggle free with one hand as he held his torch up with the other.

"The toilet," said Divina and Molly together.

"Well whatever it is, it's all slimy and my feet can't feel the bottom."

"That's because toilets don't have bottoms," said Divina.

"They do sometimes have bottoms," said Molly. "That's what toilets are for."

"Never mind all that," said Urgum. "This toy-lett thing is swallowing me."

On the wall next to him was a very very long strip of skin wound up into a roll. Urgum grabbed the loose end, but as he tried to pull himself out of the hole, the roll unwound and he slipped further in. Molly dashed forward, snatched the roll from the wall and pulled with all her might. But just as Urgum was starting to ease out of the hole, the skin ripped.

"Waahhhh!" cried Urgum as he disappeared down through the floor, still clutching his flaming torch.

"Ooops," said Molly and Divina.

THUMP

KLUMP BLUMP

Urgum found himself sliding and rolling down a long dark shaft, as he held on to the torch. With his free hand, he tried to grab the side and stop himself, but the rock was too slippery and over he tumbled. Suddenly, the bottom of the shaft disappeared completely and he fell through space to land *SPLATT* in an utterly putrid pond of filth.

At least he'd stopped moving and luckily his torch was still alight. He sat up, with the mess lapping round his waist, and looked around. He was in a small, circular cavern with smooth walls that glistened in the torchlight. High above him was the dark hole in the roof he'd fallen through, and it was clear that there was no way of getting back up there.

Urgum sighed and wondered how he was going to die. Starvation? Unlikely. Drowning? Not if he could help it. Boredom? Possibly, but by far the most likely thing to kill him was the smell. If ever there was a place that smelt completely opposite to the kitchen, this was it. The atmosphere in the cavern was so thick, he could have cut off a couple of slices and mended his boots with them.

And then, just as he'd decided that things couldn't get any worse, he felt something with fingers grab hold of his ankle beneath the surface of the pond.

Despite being the bravest and most vicious savage that the Lost Desert had ever known, Urgum ripped himself free and scrambled back towards the cavern wall. Behind him, the putrid liquid bubbled and then, slowly, a hideous stinking creature rose up out of the mire. It seemed to be of human shape but was matted in dripping filth. It staggered to its feet and wiped its eye sockets with the back of its hands. Cautiously, the two eyes blinked open and focused on the torch in surprise. After a bit more wiping the face became visible, and then the mouth began to splutter and spit. Finally the creature spoke.

"Oh hello, Urgum," it said. "How's things?"

How Hunjah Lost His Head

Urgum stared aghast at his unexpected companion. Of course, he should have realized what all this was about: the disappearing builder, the spoon, the toy-lett, the creature in the filth...

"Oh no!" Urgum sighed. "Not Hunjah!"

"Sorry it's taking me so long to finish the toilet," said Hunjah, holding up a little piece of twisted metal. "But the end broke off my spoon."

Through the gloom and the stench-fumes, Urgum looked at the patheticest barbarian that had ever lived.

"Hunjah!" he said, exasperated. "What did you have to dig this dirty big long stinky slimy black hell of a hole for?"

"It's the toilet drain," said Hunjah. "But it got a bit dark down here, so while I was digging away I must have taken a wrong turning."

"How do we get out?" asked Urgum. "The walls are too slimy to climb."

"That's the tricky bit," admitted Hunjah. "I keep hoping I'll dig through the rock and come out somewhere. What's that on your arm?"

"Mungoid's battle teeth," said Urgum, who had forgotten they were there. "They've locked on."

"Pity," said Hunjah. "They could have gnashed through the rock in no time."

"Can't help that," said Urgum. "Mungoid said that I need a bit of twisted metal like a broken spoon to get them off. Where am I going to get a broken spoon down here?"

"No idea," said Hunjah. "I've got one, it's just a shame you haven't."

"Then we'll just have to sit here in the bottom of this toy-lett until we die," said Urgum. "Not much of a death for the savagest barbarian that ever lived."

"Not even much of a death for the patheticest barbarian that ever lived," said Hunjah. "Still, you have to laugh, haven't you?"

"No," said Urgum.

So they sat there not laughing.

Meanwhile, up in the main part of the cave, the boys were sitting round eating some of the burnt bits from the outside of the giraffe. Luckily for Divina, none of her sons had inherited their father's legendary appetite, and the main part of the dinner was still intact. Even luckier, they were exhausted and she knew that once they were full they would fall asleep. Thank goodness that her guests would not have to witness the boys' table manners.

"There's just one more bit left," announced Molly from the kitchen entrance. With a finger and thumb she dangled one last piece of tasty burnt giraffe leg in front of them. "Who wants it?"

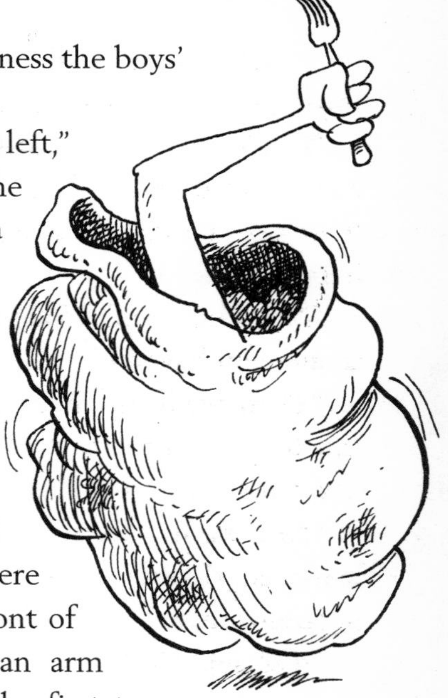

"ME!" shouted six of the boys, getting up and rushing towards her. But there was a bag on the floor in front of them, and out of it shot an arm clutching a fork. Ruff was the first to try and get past, but the arm stabbed the fork hard into his knee and he fell back, yelping, knocking the others over behind him. Ruinn managed to fight his way to the top of the pile of bodies, but when he tried to crawl free and get over to Molly he found the fork was being held in front of his face, all ready to poke out his eyeball. Very carefully, he retreated again.

"It's all yours then, Raymond," said Molly reaching

down and sticking the meat on the fork. With a nimble vault the arm leapt over to another bag and deposited the meat inside.

CHOMP CHOMP **BURP**

went the second bag.

With the meal finished, it wasn't long before the boys had all dragged themselves into their new room, and soon a chorus of satisfied snores was coming out of it. Divina went to stand at the entrance to the cave and stare out across Golgarth basin. As night had fallen, her teeth had bitten down further and further into her lower lip. Molly came out to join her.

"Are your posh friends here yet?" she asked, peering into the darkness.

"No they are not here yet," snapped Divina.

"Then why can't we pull Dad out of the toilet?"

"It serves him right for making me wait ten years for him. Besides, I don't want my lady friends meeting him."

"But you were expecting them ages ago," said Molly. "They're very late."

"Well of course they are," replied Divina. "These are very grand ladies and according to *Modern Savage* magazine, only servants should arrive on time. The grander you are, the later you should turn up."

"Dad was ten years late," said Molly. "That means he must be really grand. So why are you leaving him down the toilet?"

"That's enough, Molly. Go and make sure the giraffe's still burning properly."

"If your grand ladies are late enough, can I help you put them down the toilet too?"

"MOLLY!"

Molly wasn't sure if this meant yes or no, but she hoped it meant yes. She went in to check the dinner.

Down in the stinky cavern, things hadn't progressed much. Urgum was tugging at Mungoid's battle teeth, but they still wouldn't come off his arm.

"Oh, if only I had a broken spoon," he moaned.

"Yes." Hunjah fiddled with his broken spoon. "It's certainly a pity."

"Look at that those two idiots!" screamed another voice, but neither Urgum nor Hunjah heard it...

Up in the Halls of Sirrus, the laughter had come to a stop. Instead, the barbarian gods were looking down on Urgum and going mad with frustration.

"Why doesn't Urgum just borrow Hunjah's broken spoon?" said Tangor. "It's bad enough that he nearly kills himself riding round the Forgotten Crater, but now he's quietly waiting to die stuck down the bottom of a toilet!"

"The other gods will love this!" moaned Tangal. "They'll laugh themselves silly at us."

"It's your fault," said her brother. "If you hadn't had your little joke and moved everything on ten years, Divina wouldn't have had time to put this toilet in."

"How was I to know he'd go and throw himself down it?" said Tangal. "Now come on, we'd better get down there and do something."

And so, unknown to Urgum and Hunjah, they were joined in the cavern by two spiritual beings. Disguised as fleas, they hovered together just outside Urgum's left ear.

"Urgum!" whispered Tangal into the ear. "Ask Hunjah if you can borrow his spoo ... mmph!"

Tangor slapped his little flea hand across his sister's mouth and hurriedly dragged her away. He was just in time. The buzzing noise of Tangal's tiny whisper had made Urgum stick his finger in his ear and wiggle it about.

"What's the idea?" demanded Tangal.

"I've just realized!" said Tangor. "Urgum can't ask to borrow a broken spoon to save his life! It would be like begging for mercy."

"You're right!" Tangal gasped. "Think of the shame if our last true barbarian started begging for mercy. The other gods would laugh at us."

"So what do we do?" said her brother helplessly. "Either he borrows the spoon, or ... our last true barbarian dies at the bottom of an unfinished toilet, and then there's no one left to believe in us so we stop being proper gods and *then* he arrives at our table and we have to feed him for all eternity!"

"We have to let him die at the bottom of the unfinished toilet," Tangal admitted. "It's the only honourable thing to do."

"An honourable death down the toilet," muttered Tangor sarcastically. "You know what, sister? This joke you played on Urgum truly stinks."

But the words Tangal whispered to Urgum had sunk deeper into his brain than the gods realized. Horrified, they watched Urgum turn to Hunjah...

"Hunjah," said Urgum. "Can I borrow your spoommph?"

"My what?" asked Hunjah.

"Maybe not spoommph," said Urgum. "Spoof maybe? Have you got a spoof?"

"No," said Hunjah.

"Oh well," said Urgum. "Never mind then."

The gods breathed in a sigh of relief.

"GOTTIT!" cried Urgum triumphantly.

The gods breathed out their sigh of relief and swapped it for a sigh of depair.

"Got what?" asked Hunjah.

"I've just had a brilliant idea!" said Urgum pointing at Hunjah's broken spoon. "You've got a broken spoon..."

"Correct."

"...and I need a broken spoon to get Mungoid's teeth off my arm..."

"...true..."

Urgum beamed. "So, can I borrow your broken spoon?"

"Er..." said Hunjah, looking at his broken spoon.

"I don't want to hear this!" said Tangor to Tangal who had already stuck her tiny flea feet into her tiny flea ears so she didn't hear him.

"...no," said Hunjah.

"WHAT?" shouted Urgum.

“I said no.”

“Hurrah for Hunjah!” The gods cheered. “He has saved Urgum’s honour! Oh, happy day.”

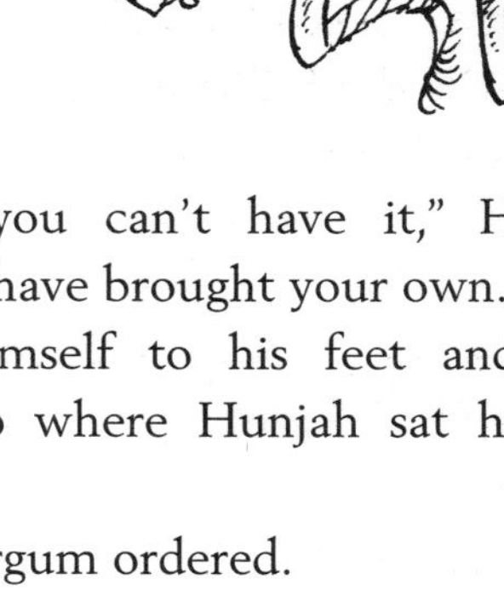

“WHY?” Urgum demanded.

“It’s mine and you can’t have it,” Hunjah replied. “You should have brought your own.”

Urgum raised himself to his feet and splashed through the filth to where Hunjah sat hugging his broken spoon.

“On your feet,” Urgum ordered.

“W ... what for?” said Hunjah getting up and backing away.

“Because I’m about to flatten you.” Urgum snarled, raised a mighty fist and drew it back to his shoulder.

“Tangor, quick!” hissed Tangal. “Power to his arm!”

And so when Urgum drove his fist at Hunjah’s face, the two gods were sitting on his knuckles, adding their divine force to increase his strike power a thousand times over. Hunjah's head flew clean away from his shoulders and smacked against the cavern wall.

KLABBUNCH!

With a splosh it fell into the filth, the eyes still blinking in confusion. Urgum pulled back his arm and examined his fist. He'd smacked it into lots of things but it had never felt as good as that!

"Wow Hunjah," said Urgum. "Did you see that?"

Then he realized that Hunjah wasn't really in a position to answer which was a shame. When you throw a punch as good as that, you like somebody to go and tell everybody else about it, even if it's only Hunjah.

... a few fragments of rock fell from the wall where the head had hit it and splashed into the putrid pond. Attracted by the noise Urgum looked up in time to see bigger and bigger bits of rock starting to fall, and then, with a great rumble, the whole side of the cavern collapsed. Urgum found himself looking through a large hole at the night sky. A welcome gush of clean air came in and filled his nose, and the filth in the pond started to flow away from around his feet and out through the crack in the wall.

"Urgum is saved!" Tangor cheered.

"And his honour is intact," said Tangal. "And it's all thanks to Hunjah."

The gods looked down to the floor, where Hunjah's eyes were finally fluttering shut under the yellowy surface of the pond.

"We should give him another chance," said Tangal.

Tangor nodded in agreement so, as Urgum leant out of the hole and took in gulps of clean night air, a most curious thing happened behind his back. Hunjah's headless corpse got on to its knees, then crawled around with the hands feeling their way in the ebbing puddle. Soon, the fingers closed around the head, lifted it up and plonked it back on to the neck with a dull squelch. A couple of twists had it facing roughly the right way,

then the eyes blinked open and the mouth yawned.

Urgum was still refreshing his lungs by the hole when he felt a tap on his shoulder. He looked around to see Hunjah holding his head on with one hand and offering the broken spoon with the other. Around his neck a ragged line dripped with filth. Urgum knew that he ought to be terrified out of his mind or, at the very least, feeling a mixture of astonishment and disgust. But frankly, after everything else that had been happening, he just couldn't be bothered.

"What do you want now?" he asked.

"If you're going to be touchy, then OK, you can borrow my broken spoon. But don't be too rough, I don't want you to break it."

Urgum sighed in disbelief. It occurred to him that in some ways it must be harder to be the patheticest barbarian that ever lived than the fiercest.

"Come on, Hunjah," he said. "It's time to get you out of here."

The hole in the wall turned out to be halfway up a cliff face around the back of the cragg, and when they looked out, Urgum and Hunjah realized they were staring out across the starlit desert. Looking down (with Hunjah holding his head on), they saw one of the paths leading round to the entrance of the cragg, immediately beneath them. They scrambled out of the cavern and carefully picked their way down the shadowy rocks towards the ground.

Behind them, Tangor and Tangal cheered the unexpected success of their mission and dematerialized back up to Sirrus to celebrate with a divine-size pizza (which is slightly bigger than a continent and yet slightly smaller than a gnat's wing – being supernatural is great fun, but also very confusing).

At last, Urgum and Hunjah reached the path.

"You OK?" Urgum asked.

"I think so," said Hunjah. "I'll get a new spoon and come back and finish the job tomorrow."

"It's fine as it is," said Urgum. "Now off you go. It's late."

"See you then," said Hunjah. "Oh, and by the way, thanks for saving my life."

"Eh?"

"You came down the toilet to rescue me!" said Hunjah. "Don't say you've forgotten already? Not many people would have risked their lives for someone as pathetic as me. You're a true hero."

"Er ... don't mention it," muttered Urgum, feeling rather embarrassed.

"In another couple of years I might have died down there. I owe you a big favour."

"No you don't," Urgum insisted.

"Really?" said Hunjah. "Oh good. In that case I'll just send you my bill for the building work then."

"No you won't," said Urgum hurriedly.

"Won't I?"

"No! I came down the toilet especially to save your life remember? You owe me a favour."

"But you said..."

"BYE-BYE, HUNJAH."

Hunjah toddled off into the night but, as Urgum watched him go, he realized that something wasn't quite right.

"All that stinky stuff I was sitting in," thought Urgum, looking all around him. "Where did it go?"

Sure enough, there were a few damp patches on the pathway beneath the hole in the cliff, but most of the mess that had flowed out from the stinky cavern seemed to have disappeared.

Urgum shrugged his shoulders and headed round to the cragg entrance. It was one of those mysteries he'd never know the answer to, which was a shame because, if he had known, it would have amused him mightily.

A Shock for the Ladies

At exactly the same time that Urgum was asking to borrow Hunjah's broken spoon, a very grand procession was proceeding down the path beneath the cliff face. A team of muscular slaves dressed in green and gold uniforms carried a massive sedan sofa with three of the finest ladies of the Lost Desert sitting on it.

They were the very cream of the Laplace Palace society and they were on their way to have roast giraffe and sparkling conversation with Divina.

"Silly little Divina!" Suprema giggled as she wafted herself with a cobra hood fan. "She honestly thinks she can still be as grand as us."

"Did you know, she reads that dreadful *Modern Savage* magazine?" said Glamora (with the leopard-foot earrings). "And she believes it."

"I scream to think what she's tried to do to that pokey little cave of hers," said Beautasha (with the diamond-studded eyeballs).

"And as for that pet monkey she keeps!"

"A pet monkey?"

"You know the one. She dresses it up as a girl. She calls it Molly."

The sofa heaved and creaked on the slaves' shoulders as shrieks of tinny laughter rang out, and at that moment a low rumbling noise came from the cliff face. Of course, the ladies were far too grand to notice such a trifle, but the charge-slave at the front heard it and looked upwards. The rest followed his gaze and saw the mass of stinky sludge about to cascade down over them from the cliff.

The slaves knew it was their duty to save their beloved ladies from danger, or they would be whipped with red-hot chains. The choice was obvious so, without a moment's hesitation, they dropped the sedan sofa to the ground and dived for cover just as the green sludge hit the tops of the ladies' heads. It splattered through their hair, sprayed across their faces, necks and arms and slithered right down to their dainty little ankles in their rhino-horn shoes. For a moment there was a deathly silence and then, all at once, in three-part harmony, the ladies started screaming.

When the very last drop had fallen from the cliff, the slaves approached, holding their noses, and lifted up the sedan sofa. Without waiting for orders, they turned straight round and started running to the perfume spas of Laplace Palace. Sure, the red-hot chains were going to be sore, but boy oh boy, it had been worth it.

Urgum Prepares for Dinner

It was getting late into the night and Divina still hadn't moved from the cave entrance. Beside her, Molly tossed stones at the bats flitting around a flaming torch sticking out from the rock. Beyond the pool of light, the basin was dead black.

"Maybe your ladies have had an accident, Mum," said Molly. "Or maybe they forgot."

"Go and check the dinner," snapped Divina.

"Not again!" Molly moaned. "What's the point? You know they're not coming. Why can't Dad be allowed to have some?"

Divina sniffed. "Pah! After what he said about our lovely bedroom? Oh no. If he wants to live like a savage, then he can eat like a savage. He can catch his own meat and eat it raw."

"Well he can't catch anything if he's still down the toilet," said Molly. "We ought to at least try to get him out."

"Shhh!" said Divina, suddenly peering into the darkness. "Listen, what's that?"

A few low grumbles came from the direction of the cragg entrance.

Molly sniffed the air. "Sounds like Olk's letting somebody in."

"It'll be my ladies!" exclaimed Divina excitedly.

"Wow, they really stink, don't they?" said Molly, holding her nose.

"That is not a stink!" replied Divina. "That will be their sweet perfumes." She took a deep sniff, and then fell over coughing, spitting and clutching her stomach.

"I warned you those ladies really stink." Molly laughed.

Divina spluttered. "What ... whatever that is, it is

NOT my ladies and I don't want it here."

"I'll go and chase it away," said Molly.

"STOP!" ordered Divina. "What kind of a mother would let an unarmed girl walk round Golgarth basin in the black of night?"

"You mean I can't go out?" said Molly.

"I mean there might be wild animals out there." Divina passed Molly a huge spiked club. "So take this and try to catch something for breakfast."

"Wow, super!" Molly grinned.

She set out across the basin in the dark, swinging the club round her head, hoping to hit something. She heard a shuffling noise on the far rocks and as she crossed the basin towards it the smell got stronger. With a bit of luck it would be a sabre-toothed skunk. They were always good for a fight, even if they did stink more than anything else in the Lost Desert. But in the end the stinky thing stank even more than the stinkiest sabre-toothed skunk ever stunk.

"Of course you can stay here!"

Molly heard Mungoid's distant voice in the dark, then saw the Ungoid himself bring a flaming torch and a broken spoon out from his cave. Urgum was sitting on his steps. Mungoid sat beside him and started to unlock the battle teeth and prise them out of his arm.

"Thanks, old friend, I just need somewhere to put my head down." Urgum wiggled his fingers as the great jaws of the battle teeth eased open slightly. "You know what it's like when you're on a hunting party. I haven't slept for months."

"Er, yes. And when I say you can stay here, of course I mean that you *could* stay here, but it's just that..."

"It's just that ... what?"

"I don't know quite how to put this," said Mungoid cautiously, but luckily assistance was at hand.

A voice from the next cave entrance shrieked, "What is that gut-gouging, bottom-burning, vulture-vomit of a smell?"

Mungoid looked round and instinctively combed his banana-sized fingers over his three hairs. "Thank you

Grizelda!" he called back. He turned back to Urgum. "Yes, that's the best way of putting it. She's rather good with words, don't you think?"

"Since when has a healthy bit of scent bothered you?" asked Urgum.

"Me?" Mungoid laughed. "Hah! It doesn't bother me. It's just that these days, occasionally there might be the chance of a bit of company..."

Mungoid gazed wistfully through the darkness in the direction of Grizelda's cave.

"So you're saying I need a wash then?"

Mungoid hurriedly turned his concentration back to retrieving the battle teeth from Urgum's arm. No way was he going to say "yes" until he was ready to defend himself. After all, Divina was the only person who'd ever made Urgum have a wash and lived to talk about it. (This was such a nasty event that if anyone were to hear about it, they'd be sick.)

"I said: are you saying I need a wash?" Urgum repeated.

KUDDONK!

The teeth were free. Mungoid quickly put them in his mouth and stood up. He clashed his jaws together a couple of times to check they were ready for a superb fight, then took a couple of steps over to where a small pool of water nestled amongst the rocks. Taking a deep breath, Mungoid pointed at the pool, and nodded.

"To the death!" Urgum snarled, leaping to his feet.

"Chew the death!" repeated Mungoid, trying to control his teeth. But then he added, "Are you shure? You haven't goth your acksh. Don't you want to go and geth it firtht?"

"I'm not going back to my cave," said Urgum. "I'll just pretend I've got it. Swish swish chop. Well come on, attack me back then!"

"But you'll jush geth chomped to biths," said Mungoid. "And then ... you'll be dead."

Urgum's shoulders slumped and he sighed wearily. "Maybe it's for the best," he said. "I don't fit in round here any more. Did you know that our cave's suddenly got a lee-ow-un-je and cushions? It's turned into some sickly sort of girl world. And I can't impose on you, old friend, I don't want to cramp your style with the ladies. I've run out of options. There's only one place left where this old savage will be welcome now."

Urgum raised his eyes towards the black night sky where a few stars twinkled brightly and the rest just hung around looking bored. With his chin out and shoulders proudly back, he beat his arms across his chest.

"TANGOR! TANGAL!" he cried, in a voice loud enough to reach the far side of the darkness. "Oh immortal twins, I call upon you to welcome your servant Urgum to the hallowed Halls of Sirrus. I have lived as your true champion and so come now to sit between you at your table, there to feast upon the divine nectar of the gods for eternity."

Urgum hadn't picked the best time for this announcement because, up in the Halls of Sirrus, the barbarian gods were relaxing after their trip down the toilet drain. Tangor was leaning back in his great marble chair and taking a nap with his feet up on one end of the table. At the other end of the table, Tangal was using a large basin of water to wash her hair. Between them was a pizza box, slightly bigger than a continent and yet slightly smaller than a gnat's wing, and all around them was a happy scattering of crusts, crumbs and spat-out anchovies.

Tangal had just been reaching for a towel when she caught the end of Urgum's speech and went into a blind panic.

"Wake up, Tangor!" she shouted. "Urgum's preparing to die, and he's on his way up here!"

"Eh?" Tangor rubbed his eyes. "He can't be dying again, we've only just saved him. This better not be another of your jokes."

"No joke," insisted Tangal. "He definitely said he's on his way to feast at our table for eternity. He's even planned where he's going to sit for goodness' sake, he wants to be in the middle. We'll need to get a third chair from somewhere. But first, get the washing up done."

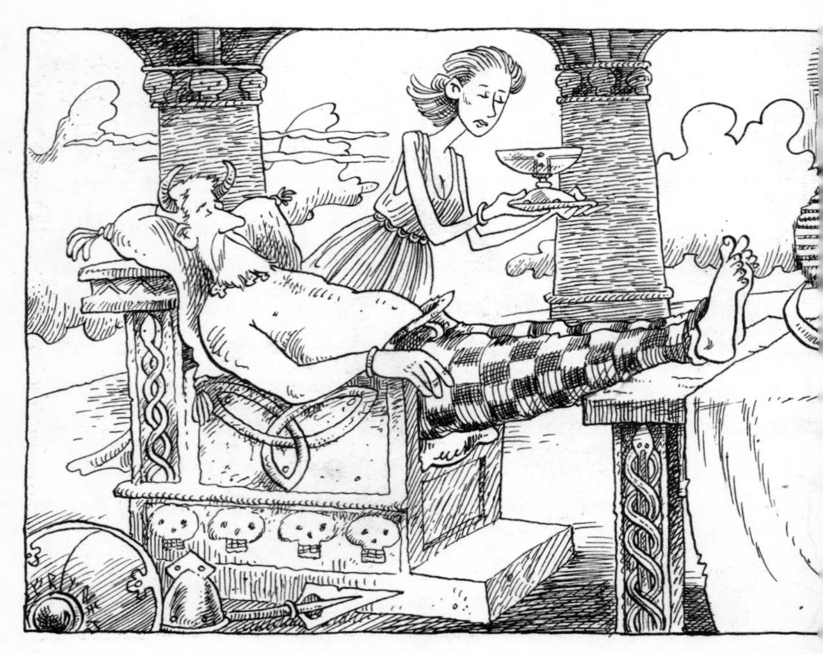

"It's not my turn."

"And when you've done that, we need some nectar. Get rid of this pizza box and nip out for a couple of jars of nectar, and he wants the divine stuff, so don't get that cheap one that tastes like mashed turnip."

"Oh no! He sounds even fussier than his father was. Why have we got to do this just for Urgum?"

"You know very well why!" Tangal rubbed her head furiously with a towel. "Because we're gods and it's what he expects! If he didn't believe in us then we

wouldn't exist! Now hurry. Wash up, dump the pizza box, get the nectar, and put your new sandals on, those ones are filthy. And don't forget the chair."

"But why aren't you doing anything?"

"I am! I'm drying my hair. Now get moving."

Meanwhile, in the terrestial world, Molly had seen enough. As Urgum prepared himself to be gnashed to death by Mungoid's terrible battle teeth, she ran between them shouting, "Dad! What are you doing?"

"I'm having a fight to the death with Mungoid," said Urgum.

"Well at least defend yourself!" Molly thrust the club Divina had given her into his hands.

Urgum raised it and with a snarl, he turned towards Mungoid. But then he let the club drop back to his side. He tossed it away into the night and shrugged. "Thanks Molly, but I'm not in the mood for defending. So goodbye for ever and take care of your mum. She's a good woman."

"You can't die!" said Molly. "You're Urgum the Axeman. You're a legend, you're supposed to live for ever."

"But Molly," replied Urgum wearily. "As everybody

keeps telling me ... things have changed!"

"Aw, Urgum," said Mungoid. "Are you shure about thith?"

Mungoid had been looking forward to giving his new teeth a really good test, but not on his unarmed best friend. It didn't seem right somehow.

"If you call yourself my friend, you'll do it," said Urgum. "Come on and make it as savage and bloody as you can. I want to die in a truly horrific manner, suitable for the fiercest barbarian that ever lived. Let's be having those teeth of yours in me."

"I've only jush goth them outh of you!"

"Then it's time to put them back in again, isn't it?"

Urgum bent over and turned his rear end towards Mungoid.

"I'll make it easy for both of us," he said. "Start here: I can still feel where that cushion hugged me. Yuk! Put me out of my misery."

But Molly could stand it no longer. She ran up to Urgum's

rough old face and clasped his cheeks in her hands.

"DAD, NO!" she shouted.

Urgum gazed down sadly at the girl. She looked back up at her long-lost father in his last moments before being minced to an agonizing death by the Ungoid battle teeth. Did she cry? Did she tremble? No, she drew her fist back and punched him in the mouth.

"Wow!" said Urgum, impressed, followed quickly by, "Yow! What was that for?"

"I've been waiting ten years for my brave savage father to come home and teach me how to be a barbarian. But now you're here, you've decided that you'd rather die by having your bottom bitten to bits. How selfish can you get?"

"Sho do you want me to kill him or noth?" asked Mungoid who'd got rather confused.

"You dare and I'll punch your face as well," said Molly.

"Ignore her," said Urgum to Mungoid. "Go ahead, kill me now. Go on, get chomping."

"But I don't want a punsh!" said Mungoid. "Punsh's are shore."

With a creak and a plop Mungoid tugged the battle teeth out of his mouth and sat down on his steps. He was really grateful that Molly had given him an excuse not to chew Urgum to death.

"Thank you Mungoid," said Molly. "Now come on, Dad." She grabbed Urgum's hand and started to haul him away.

"Where are we going?" asked Urgum, dragging his feet.

"Home."

They were almost back at their cave when Urgum dug his heels in and halted. Divina was still standing under the blazing torch at the cave entrance and trying to look like she couldn't care less.

"That isn't my home," said Urgum. "My home doesn't have a lee-ow-un-je and a toy-lett."

"Mum!" called Molly. "I've found Dad!"

"Pooh! I can tell!" said Divina. "What's he doing there? I thought he was down the toilet."

"He's tired and hungry, so invite him in," said Molly.

"Maybe he doesn't want to come in," said Divina. "He made it quite plain he doesn't like what I've done. Well, if he wants to live like a savage, let him go and live like one."

"You see, Molly?" said Urgum. "That's not my home. Full of cushions and silks and lee-ow-un-jes. Your mother's worked hard to improve the place, she doesn't need a smelly old savage ruining it for her. All this modern living, I don't fit in."

"Of course you do!" said Molly.

"No," said Urgum. "And she's got her posh friends coming, I'd just make her feel awkward."

"Tell him, Mum."

"Tell him what?"

"Tell him your posh friends aren't coming because you know they're not. It's almost the middle of the night."

Divina turned her back on them, but Molly hadn't finished.

"And tell him that your friends are really horrible and boring. You'd rather have him. Go on, he's waiting."

"I'm telling him nothing," said Divina. "He doesn't deserve to be talked to while he's in that stinky filthy state."

"See?" said Urgum. "I'm going back to Mungoid. At least I've tried."

"No you haven't tried!" cried Molly. "Neither of you have! This is SO STUPID. We can't be a nice family all together because of a little bit of dirt. Is that right?"

There was an embarrassed silence. Urgum stared at the ground, Divina's feet twitched uncomfortably. Molly heaved a great sigh of frustration then shouted across to where Mungoid was watching:

"Mungoid, bring us some water."

Mungoid didn't think it was a good idea, but at the same time, he was too far away to follow exactly what was going on. It had been a long time since he'd seen

Urgum and Divina have a really good row, and he didn't want to miss it, so he hurriedly filled a clam shell from his rock pool and brought it over.

"All right Dad," said Molly. "You know what to do."

"What?" muttered Urgum, looking crossly into Mungoid's clam shell.

"Have a wash," said Molly.

There was a stunned silence because Divina was the

only person who'd ever made Urgum have a wash and lived. (This was such a nasty event that if anyone were to hear about it, they'd be sick.)

"Well?" demanded Molly, who got bored very quickly with stunned silences. "Is my big brave father scared of a little bit of water? Because I'm not."

Molly leant her head over the shell and splashed some water into her face.

"See?" she said. "Is that *so* difficult?"

Molly stood back and beckoned Urgum towards the shell.

"Well go on then," Molly ordered. "It's your turn! Go on, do it for Mum's sake."

Urgum slowly approached Mungoid, who held the shell out at arm's length. Mungoid had no idea what might happen. Urgum could smash the shell, he could smash Mungoid, he could smash Mungoid with the shell... Mungoid shut his eyes and braced himself for the unexpected.

Splibble splish splottle

Mungoid opened his eyes to see Urgum dabbling the very ends of his fingertips into the water. He certainly hadn't expected that.

"He won't do it," Divina sneered. "I know he won't."

Urgum looked her straight in the eye and then applied one damp finger end to each of his cheeks and gave a little rub.

Mungoid gasped. "You ... you had a wash!"

"Yes! Well, you see..." said Urgum, "...things have changed."

Divina launched herself at him and threw her arms around his neck.

"Oh Urgum, you're such a big smoothie!" she gushed and kissed him right on the nose.

Before Urgum had a chance to understand what was happening, Divina and Molly were dragging him towards their cave.

"My poor darling, you must be starving!" Divina said. "Come on in, Urgie, and loosen your belt."

"And Robbin made some orange sauce, Dad!" said Molly. "You'll like it."

"Oranges?" Urgum was now utterly confused. "You mean you've been cooking oranges like the same oranges that come off a tree? Don't they taste of wood?"

"No!" Molly giggled. "You'll love it, honest."

As the three of them tumbled happily into their cave entrance, Mungoid was left out on his own, clutching the clam shell. With a sigh, he started to head back towards his own empty cave and so didn't quite catch the conversation that was drifting his way.

"Mum," said Molly. "As your friends aren't coming, can I bring a friend to tea?"

"I suppose so," replied Divina. "But who?"

Molly's head reappeared at the cave entrance.

"MUNGOID!" she yelled back across the basin.

The big ugly barbarian stopped in his tracks and looked round hopefully.

"Well don't just stand there," she shouted. "Are you coming in?"

Unsweet Dreams

One massive blow-out gargantuan meal with orange sauce later...

"I don't want to go to bed." Urgum yawned. "I'm not tired."

"You're not still moaning about the bedroom, are you?" asked Divina.

"But it's so sickly," complained Urgum. "I'll have nightmares about skipping through fields of flowers with ribbons in my hair!"

"Yes, I was thinking about that," said Molly. "So come with me, Dad. I've made a little change. I think you'll like it."

Molly dragged Urgum down the corridor and pushed him through the archway into the bedroom. Urgum stood there blinking uncertainly as the burning torchlight flickered around the room. The walls and ceiling were still covered in cascades of shimmering silk, the floor was still quilted in a patchwork of tasselled cushions, a white marble table was still overloaded with pots of make-up; dresses and shawls were still hanging from wall hooks and towering urns of flowers still filled every corner. In fact Urgum was just about to throw up until he spotted what Molly had done.

"Well, Dad?" asked Molly. "What do you think?"

A huge smile crossed his craggy face.

"Did you do that?" asked Urgum.

Molly nodded. "I've been dying to do that since I first saw it."

"But you're supposed to be a girl!" he exclaimed.

"But I'm not just any girl," said Molly. "I'm Urgum the Axeman's girl."

"You know what?" Urgum grinned. "I'm starting to believe you are."

Then slowly his eyes closed and finally the weary warrior allowed himself to fall backwards flat on to the bed. Above him hanging from a small rope, newly dressed in a bloodstained vest and clutching a little axe was the rosy-cheeked ragdoll.

Far up in the Halls of Sirrus, Tangor and Tangal were breathless. The room was spotless, they'd borrowed a chair, the divine nectar was heating up in the cauldron, the table was clear and Tangor's sandals and Tangal's hair were immaculate.

"So when's he coming?" said Tangor impatiently.

"Should be any time now," said Tangal. "I wish he'd given us more notice."

"Hang on," said Tangor suspiciously. "What's that sound?"

They became aware of a strange rumbling noise from the flower-filled bedroom, far down below in the terrestrial world.

"It's Urgum!" said Tangor. "And he's snoring!"

"Well, of all the cheek!" snapped Tangal. "I thought he was dying."

Although Urgum hadn't died, he didn't wake up for nine days. Barbarians work hard and play hard. And when they finally get home, they sleep hard.

Some things don't change.

PART THREE
The Footprint in the Flower Bed

The Savage and the Softhand II

When Urgum finally woke up and saw the new bedroom and realized it hadn't all been a weird dream he did a big scream.

"ARGHHHHHHHH!"

Molly heard him and came to see what the matter was. Urgum took one look at her and realized that she was real too and did another big scream.

"ARGHHHHHHHH!"

He jumped out of the four-poster bed with the intention of ripping everything he could see to tiny pieces, but his great axe was lying on the ground and he rammed his big toe on to the blade and split it in two down the middle.

"ARGHHHHHHH!"

Urgum fell to the floor and sat there sucking his toe, which luckily stopped any more screaming coming out.

"Have you *quite* finished?" Molly asked. "Because if you have, I'll show you a secret."

Urgum was secretly rather pleased that he was being shown a secret, and changed his mind about ripping everything to pieces. He hobbled through to Molly's room and watched as she rolled back the pink fluffy rug on the floor. Underneath it was a little hole. She reached into it and pulled out a small piece of velvet cloth that was folded around something. She unwrapped it and showed her father what was inside.

"Is that ... money?" asked Urgum.

"Of course it is," said Divina over his shoulder, making him jump. "They're real bronze tannas, and she earnt them herself by making necklaces and bracelets with her flowers. Isn't she a clever girl?"

Urgum looked at the small pile of bronze circles and tried to be impressed.

"So explain this to me," he said. "You spend days and days growing your little flowers, then you pick them and make little necklaces and things, and *then* you sit around for more days hoping somebody will come past and give you some of those coin money things for them?"

"That's it!" said Molly.

"Why?" asked Urgum.

"Because it's money, Urgum!" said Divina. "You can buy things with it."

"So what are you going to buy?"

"Ah!" Molly grinned. "That's a secret."

"Huh," said Urgum, sulking. "So you've shown me your secret, but after all that, it's still a secret. It's horrible sneaky stuff is money. I hate it."

And with that he hobbled off away down the corridor. Molly was about to protest, but then saw that her mother was shaking her head, indicating that it wasn't worth the effort. Molly carefully hid her coins again, and then got out her spade and started sorting some seeds out. She didn't care what her grumpy old dad thought, she liked growing her flowers and was very proud when she managed to sell them, even if she had no idea what to use the money for.

Divina stood in the doorway, watching her, thinking back to when she'd first met Urgum, all those years ago. He'd made his feelings about money *very* clear...

Of course, when she'd called him a wimp, after he'd just disabled six armed slaves with only an axe handle, she'd meant it as a joke, but even before the word had travelled the short distance between her mouth and his ears, she was regretting it. Although it would have been regarded as the height of sophisticated wit if they'd all been sitting round at a softhand tea party, Divina realized that in the real world, where people had to fight for survival, those nasty little remarks weren't so funny after all.

She straightened her shoulders and prepared herself for the horrible death that she knew she deserved from the insulted savage. *Oh well,* she thought, *let's try and face this with a bit of dignity,* and so she just kept her mouth clamped shut and stared at him waiting for the worst to happen.

To her surprise, the savage seemed so gobsmacked at being stared at that he just stood frozen to the spot, staring back. Divina felt stangely exhilarated by this, or at least she would have done if it hadn't been for her father beside her, who was fidgeting nervously and muttering cowardly threats under his breath.

After a while, she knew that if she had to listen to him whisper the words "doesn't-that-oxbrain-realize-who-I-am?" one more time, she would hurl herself on to the nearest sword point, so instead she decided to get up and try to do something helpful in the last moments before she died.

From the ground near the sofa, the groans of the

injured slaves had been gradually getting louder, so Divina picked up a water urn and went to offer it round. She heard her father making shocked noises ("...to think a girl of mine would go round serving a bunch of worthless slaves? Oh the shame...") but she didn't care. It was very rare that the privileged daughter of a softhand got to show a true act of kindness, and she was glad she'd had a chance to make a few poor souls feel slightly better before she died. As she knelt beside one of them to wipe the blood from his smashed mouth, she stole a quick glance back at the savage. He still hadn't moved, he was just staring at her in undisguised admiration. She had no idea why this should be, but she was thrilled and she wanted this instant to last for ever, and so naturally that's when her father completely ruined it.

"Look here you savage," said Gastan, trying to sound superior. He tipped some bright coins from a small bag into his hand and offered them to Urgum. "Here's some money. They're gold tannas, worth more than anything you've ever seen before, so why don't you just take it and go?"

At that moment Divina could have happily killed her father. As much as she loved him, this was one of those moments when she thought she'd prefer to be the sobbing daughter by his graveside than have to put up with him in real life.

The barbarian slowly dragged his gaze away from Divina then strode up to her father and grabbed the entire bag of coins from his hand.

The old man gasped, outraged. "What are you doing? I already offered you more than you would know how to spend in your lifetime!"

Divina trembled, but not because she was frightened. She was so full of rage and embarrassment that she had to dig her fingernails into the palms of her hands to control herself. "Shut up, Father!" she silently wished. "Shut up and shut up. Please please please just shut your shutting shut up shut."

But Gastan didn't get the message. In front of him, the barbarian was holding the bag of coins up to his face and poking it with his finger.

"Oh very well, take it all." Gastan sniffed, waving his hand dismissively. Then, with a note of triumph in his voice, he called over to Divina. "You see? These people might think they're so marvellous, but they can always be bought off."

And that was the last thing Gastan said for a while because the barbarian grabbed the back of his neck with one hand, and rammed the whole bag of coins right into Gastan's mouth with the other. It was the coolest gesture Divina had ever seen.

"Don't you want it?" she said.

"NO!"

boomed the savage. He whistled for his horse, which was

standing in the distance sniffing some grass. The horse looked up to show it had heard him, then looked away again to make it clear that it was ignoring him.

"But it's money!" said Divina. "You should take it, it'd serve him right."

"What do I want money for?" said the savage. "Lots of metal circles with faces on? What good is it in the Lost Desert? You can't fight with it, you can't eat it."

"But you can buy anything you want with money," said the girl.

"And what kind of a life would that be?" the savage sneered. "Sitting around with a pile of money just buying things? That's the trouble with you softhands, you just sit around talking and reading and writing and buying and you never actually DO anything."

"There must be something you want that money could buy you," said Divina.

To her surprise, the savage shook his head and tried to look away, but she was convinced that under the filth and the hair he was actually ... blushing!

"There is something you want!" she exclaimed. "So what is it?"

He *was* blushing! Divina tried desperately to keep a serious and respectful expression on her face in front of this terrifying and dangerous man, but it was useless. Suddenly she couldn't hold it in any more, and her face creased up into the widest and most delighted big-eyed smile that the savage had ever seen. He was so dazed by the brilliance of it that he was unable to stop looking at her until, at last, his horse got so bored of being ignored that it came over, stepped between them and shoved its bottom towards him and lashed its tail across his face.

The savage crossly walloped it out of the way, and by the time Divina could see him again his mouth had curved into a shy smile too.

"So, er ... what's your name?" he said sheepishly.

"My name?" she had asked. "You really want me to tell you my name?"

"Of course that's what I want," snapped the savage, immediately cross again. "That's why I asked. So will you tell me or have I got to buy your name with some of your money?"

"You can't buy my name!" admitted Divina. "If I don't like you, I shan't tell you it. Money won't make any difference."

"See?" said the savage. "So money can't buy what I want. So you can keep it and choke on it, the pair of you."

With that he turned his back on her and stomped off towards his horse.

"Divina!" she quickly shouted after him.

The savage stopped and turned back.

"Divina?" he repeated. "Is that your name? But I thought you weren't going to tell me."

"That was only if I didn't like you," she said.

"Oh," he said. Then after a long thought he said, "Ah."

Slowly, and slightly nervously, the savage began to wander back towards her.

And even though twenty years had passed since then, Urgum's attitude hadn't changed one tiny bit. You could offer him all the money in the world and he still wouldn't give you a bent tanna for it.

People of Laplace Palace
Hat Mocker
Insult Inventor
Ladies of the palace
Toy Collector
Matramam
Slave Prodder
Palace Guard

Arrows and Axes

The orange-flighted arrow hissed towards the sky, passing straight through the first eagle and on into the second.

WHEEE-OOO ...

THUMP

THUMP

The two birds neatly fell to earth beside Grizelda's cave entrance. Urgum was sitting on a nearby rock polishing his axe.

"There!" she annouced, triumphantly slinging her bow on to her shoulder. "What do you think of that?"

"Not much," said Urgum, sounding completely unimpressed.

He had been back home for several weeks now and this particular morning the boys had all gone off on a forage and even Mungoid had disappeared somewhere. Left with no one to fight with, Urgum had decided to amuse himself with the interesting and creative new hobby he'd taken up. In other words, he was annoying Grizelda.

"NOT MUCH?" Grizelda stomped around in front of him, pointing at the sky. "I'd like to see you pick two eagles out of the air at once with an axe."

"I wouldn't want to," said Urgum. "I don't even like eagle. They're all bone and stringy meat. And the feathers are chewy."

"Oh, get with it, Urgum!" said Grizelda. "The arrow is the modern weapon. You don't have to get close, you don't get all sweated up and dirty."

"Pah!" Urgum snorted. He ran an affectionate finger

along the handle of his axe. "Where's the satisfaction? Where's the soul? Where's the emotion? With an axe, you can feel the crunch as it goes in. With an arrow, all you get is a little 'ping'. Where's the fun in that? If you had your eyes shut you wouldn't even know if you'd hit anything or not."

"With an arrow I can hit anyone anywhere any time."

"So what?" said Urgum. "Anyone worth hitting comes over for a good fight anyway. It's very rude to kill someone you haven't met. Look, here comes Molly, we'll ask her what she thinks."

Molly had just stepped out of the cave and was heading towards the crack in the basin wall that led outside to the Lost Desert.

"Hey Molly!" called Urgum. "What's better? A nice heavy shiny axe or a pingy little arrow?"

"This is," said Molly holding up a little spade.

"Eh?" said Urgum and Grizelda.

"Killing's easy, but a spade makes things grow. Come and see my flower bed if you don't believe me." She stepped through the crack in the wall, past Olk the sentry, out and away.

"I still say axes are better," said Urgum.

"Oh really?" Grizelda pulled one of her orange-flighted arrows from the quiver on her back. "Then why don't you go and stand over by your cave and I'll stay here. We'll see who kills who first."

"I've got a better idea," said Urgum. "You stand next to me and while you're fiddling about with your bow-string, I'll chop your head off."

"Honestly!" said Grizelda. "It's so naff running about waving a big axe. Much better hiding in the shadows with a bow. I can hit someone and they don't even know who's done it."

"Oh, I see," Urgum sneered. "Don't want people to know who you are, do you? Ashamed, are you? You can't be very proud of yourself when you're pinging your little arrows at people, can you?"

By now Grizelda was getting quite cross. Urgum was enjoying himself massively.

"There's more to it than pinging arrows!" snapped Grizelda. "You can send messages, although you couldn't because you can't read or write."

"Messages?" said Urgum. "My axe sends out the only message I need: RESPECT!"

"And you can send fire arrows to burn things," said Grizelda. "Or you can poison them, or you can tie a cord on the end and set up a bridge..."

"Oh give up!" Urgum was honking with mirth. "Arrows are just a passing fad, like the wheel and eating vegetables. In a few years it'll all be over and everyone will look back at you and laugh. Me, I can't wait so I'm having my laugh now. Ho ho ho."

Grizelda was just deciding that she'd use Urgum for target practice when there was a roar from the cragg entrance.

She gasped. "That's Olk!"

"He's got trouble!" said Urgum. "Yahoo! Come on."

They both dashed to the crack in the basin wall where the massive sentry stood facing out across the desert. In the distance, thin voices screamed and jabbered.

"Yah! Useless! Missed!"

"Didn't," muttered Olk as he examined his terrible sword. A matted clump of green hair was stuck to the blade with fresh blood.

"Oh no." Grizelda sighed. "It's a gang of nappars."

Leaping about on the far rocks was a ragged group of very tall bandits with small heads and small bodies, long arms, long legs and squeaky voices. It's just as well that the nappars were proud to be the most irritating

tribe in the Lost Desert because that's what they were.

"Oversized vermin." Urgum spat. "I heard they were in the area. Looks like one of them tried to get past Olk."

Urgum and Grizelda ducked as a couple of stones flew through the air towards them. A larger stone bounced off Olk's head. The giant slowly looked up and growled as a trickle of blood oozed from the gash.

"Can't catch us!" screeched a mad voice.

Olk was about to step forwards but Urgum stopped him.

"Forget it, Olk," said Urgum. "They're too fast and not worth it. Better you stay here and keep them out. They'll move on soon."

As they watched, the nappars gradually headed off down Smiley Alley, tossing stones to knock the skulls off the stakes as they went. With a grunt, Olk pulled the clump of green hair from his blade then slapped it on his own head.

"Bandage," he explained, staring hard at Urgum and Grizelda.

"Very sensible." Urgum nodded.

"Good idea," agreed Grizelda.

"JOKE!" growled Olk, raising his massive sword.

"Oh yes, of course it is!" Grizelda laughed. "Ha ha ha, extremely funny, I must say."

"Ho ho ho!" said Urgum. "Totally hilarious. Molly would like that. Where is she, by the way?"

Olk's eyes suddenly widened in panic. With a huge finger he pointed out towards the rocks.

"Girl!" he said.

"Oh no!" cried Urgum. "She went to dig her flower bed. I'll have to get her back in case the nappars spot her."

"I'm with you," said Grizelda and together they ran out from the cragg.

Unwelcome Visitors

Under the shadow of the distant rocks, Molly was kneeling by her flower bed. It was the only patch of dark soil in the desert. Relieved to see she was alone, Urgum waved across to her and called out, "Molly! Come home quickly."

"Look at this," Molly shouted back, pointing down at the soil.

"There's no time," said Urgum.

"There is!" shouted Molly. "There's a footprint on my flower bed and I'm not happy about it."

"That doesn't matter now," said Urgum. "Come on!"

But it was too late. To his horror, a hulking figure

scrambled over the rocks and dropped down beside Molly. Grizelda was about to dash towards them, but Urgum caught her arm and dragged her behind a big clump of vegetation.

"Careful!" he whispered. "If the nappar panics and snatches her, we'll never catch him across the rocks. We need to creep up in secret."

With two swift strokes of his axe, Urgum chopped a couple of bushes from the ground and passed one to Grizelda. They dropped to their bellies and, each holding a bush in front of them, they started the long slow crawl towards the flower bed. As they got closer, they could see the bandit grinning down at Molly, who was barely taller than his knees. She was giving him a severe lecture, her cheeks crimson with fury.

"I'm warning you," she shouted, waving her spade up towards his face. "Watch where you're putting your big feet, can't you?"

"Why?" said the nappar.

"Look!" Molly pointed at the footprint. "Somebody has squashed one of my best sandroses and I'm very cross. I grew it from a seed, I watered it every day, and when the frost came I covered it in straw. Then just as it was getting a nice flower and I could sell it, it got squashed by a great big foot."

"Did it really?" The nappar sniggered. "You mean like this?"

He lifted his foot, but before he could bring it down on a second rose, Molly jumped forward and cracked his leg with the spade as hard as she could. The nappar tumbled backwards and yelped, more in surprise than pain.

"Oh dear," he said, lying on the ground and rubbing his leg. "I see you'll have to learn some respect."

"You don't scare me!" Molly stepped away from him. "I'm warning you, one day I'm going to be a barbarian."

"Pssst!" said a bush. "Over here!"

Molly looked round to see two bushes shuffling towards her.

"Don't run, just walk slowly," whispered the bush.

"What's going on?" demanded the nappar.

"Oh, it's just a talking bush," said Molly. "And it's talking to me not you, so it's none of your business."

And then a large scraggy bird swooped down from the sky.

"YEOWW!" shouted Urgum from behind the first bush, as Percy the vulture sank its claws deep into his bottom. "Get off me, you stupid bird! I'm not dead, I'm just moving very slowly!"

Grizelda leapt out from behind the second bush to dash the

last few steps towards Molly, but too late. The agile nappar had already sprung to his feet and caught Molly up under his bony arm. Although she wriggled and scratched like a burnt cat, she couldn't free herself.

"Put her down!" screamed Urgum, waving his axe with one hand and trying to pull Percy off his pants with the other.

"Make me!" The nappar laughed, and with a couple of strides he had hopped away across the rocks carrying Molly, who waved her spade helplessly. By the time Urgum got to the flower bed, they were already far out of reach. The nappar turned around and held Molly high over his head.

"Can't catch me!" he yelled.

"Dad!" shouted Molly. "Tell him I'm getting very very cross now!"

"She's getting very very cross," shouted Urgum. "And so am I."

"Oooh temper temper little girl!" said the nappar. "I'll have to teach you a lesson."

With a massive effort, Molly managed to bring her spade round and crack it across the nappar's head. To her astonishment, the bandit slowly dropped to his knees and released his grip. Molly slipped away as he fell forwards on to his face.

"Are you all right?" Urgum gasped as he clambered up the rocks towards her. "I'll chop him to bits with my axe!"

"Who needs an axe?" Molly grinned. "My spade's done a perfect job. I only gave him a small whack on the head and look."

The nappar lay there groaning as Grizelda approached clutching her bow.

"Too late, Grizelda!" Urgum laughed. "You can put that silly bow away. Molly's spade did the trick."

"Did it really?" asked Grizelda, rolling the lanky body over. Sticking out from the stomach was an orange-flighted arrow. The nappar winced in pain as Grizelda yanked it out and wiped the blood from it on to the nappar's ragged vest. "Next time I won't bother getting one of my best arrows dirty, then."

"Oh!" said Molly, disappointed. "I thought I'd knocked him out."

"Let's say it was both of us," said Grizelda. "There's only one thing for sure. It wasn't Urgum with his silly old-fashioned axe! Admit it, Urgum, you were too slow and too far away. Bows are better."

Urgum was speechless as he watched the nappar crawl away to lick his wound. He hated to admit it, but maybe Grizelda was right. After all, she had saved Molly and for that he should be grateful. He was just trying to make a sort of "You were right and I was wrong and by the way thank you very much" speech when a second nappar leapt down from an overhead ridge and landed between them. Although he was as ragged and filthy as the first, his jacket was made of a thick deep green felt. It still had a few scraps of gold braid around the cuffs which barely reached the elbows of the nappar's long scrawny arms. That jacket had once belonged to an officer in the Laplace army and for a nappar it would have been a high prize indeed. This was obviously the headnappar of the gang. The main qualities of a headnappar are high cruelty and low cunning. (Oh, and you have to be a nappar.)

"Who shot my brother?" the headnappar snarled.

"She did," said Urgum, pointing at Grizelda.

Grizelda raised her bow in defence but the headnappar brushed it aside and pinned her up against a rock with a blade to her throat. He bent down so that their noses were almost touching. Grizelda couldn't help thinking that his long teeth looked like they were made from old cheese.

"So it was you was it?" He breathed in her face. "Then you will surely die."

"Watch out, nappar." Urgum chuckled. "She's got a bow and arrow."

But the headnapper was almost leaning against Grizelda, so of course she didn't have room to load an arrow, and certainly had no space to pull back the bowstring.

"You see, Grizelda?" said Urgum. "Don't you wish you had an axe now?"

Grizelda uttered a grisly curse. She was crosser with Urgum than she was with the headnappar.

"I hate you," said Grizelda. "At least when I die I won't have to put up with you any more."

"Well that's tough because you're not going to die today," said Urgum. Holding his axe by the head, he reached up and tapped the headnappar on the shoulder with the handle.

"All right pretty boy, fun time's over," he said. "I was just trying to make a point."

"But she shot my brother," complained the headnappar, still leering horribly at Grizelda. "I demand vengeance. It's the law of the desert."

"You're telling *me* about the law of the desert?" Urgum couldn't help but laugh. "So what do you think the law says about grabbing my daughter? Your brother should be pegged out on Fire Ant Mountain so they can crawl up his nose, down his windpipe and burn his insides out. Your brother's been a lucky boy and you know it. Now buzz off before I hack you to mince."

Urgum spat on the blade of his axe and wiped his thumb around it. The razor edge glinted in the sunlight.

The nappar lowered his blade and stood back uneasily. Grizelda immediately put an arrow to her bow.

"That's your idea of a fight, is it?" the headnappar whimpered. "Two against one?"

"Three against one," said Molly. She spat on the end of her spade and wiped a bit of mud off it. "I've got a spade and I know how to use it."

"Hey Grizelda!" said Urgum. "I've had a great idea. This nappar can decide which weapon's best. Tell us, nappar, which would you rather? Either you could have a silly little arrow sticking out of you, or you could be hacked into a pile of quivering chunks by my axe."

"Or I could smack you on the leg with my spade," said Molly. "Well?"

As the three advanced on him, the headnappar backed away in panic, then tripped and landed spawling on the ground. Urgum laughed massively and said to the others, "Come on you two, we'll let him go. He's wasting my brain."

But as Urgum, Grizelda and Molly turned to leave, the headnappar called after them.

"I thought you were supposed to be Urgum the Axeman? So how come you need two girls to help you? Are you too scared to take me on alone, face to face?"

Urgum stopped in his tracks. His eyes narrowed and his knuckles went white as his fingers tightened around the axe handle. Grizelda grabbed Molly's hand and tugged her away.

"Quick, Molly!" she said. "Get right back, this could be messy."

Grizelda and Molly ran towards a tree and swung

themselves up into its branches. As they settled to watch, Urgum slowly turned back to where the headnappar was still lying. High above them two ragged black shapes were circling excitedly. For Djinta and Percy, dinner was about to be served.

"That was a mistake, nappar," growled Urgum in a voice so low that the bandit's teeth rattled. "When I told you to buzz off, you should have buzzed. Now get up and fight. If you retreat as much as one step you're dead."

Cautiously the headnappar rose to his feet, but by the time he'd straightened himself up Urgum had to tilt his head right back to look into his eyes properly.

"Happy now?" He scowled. "Now we're alone, face to face."

"No we're not," said the headnappar. "You've got your nose in my belly button."

"Doesn't bother me how big you are, you long streak of snot," said Urgum. "It's one against one. Fair enough for a fight now?"

"Fair maybe," said the headnappar. "But stupid."

"How do you mean stupid?" asked Urgum suspiciously.

Instead of replying, the headnappar tugged a buffalo horn from his belt and blew it. A strange creaking wail sounded across the stony plains. From up in the tree, Grizelda and Molly saw movement on the horizon. Six more lanky bandits had appeared and hurried over to join their leader. Urgum instinctively sidled round towards the rock wall.

"Dad!" yelled Molly from the tree. "There's seven of them now!"

"Seven?" Urgum gulped. As the nappar gang gathered in front of him he took a step backwards so that he could feel the solid rock against his shoulders. "So this is the nappar idea of fair is it?"

The headnappar grinned. "Nappars have no idea of

fair. But we have a good idea of how not to be stupid."

Urgum looked at the long leering faces. Was it true that new-born nappars are so ugly that if you pointed one at a rhinoceros herd, the whole lot would stampede off a cliff? Probably. Even the shortest nappar stood taller than Urgum. The filthy chequered dress it wore suggested that it could have been female, but the body underneath had all the feminine grace of a kebab skewer.

"Not so brave now, are you?" the headnappar sneered. "So do you want to crawl off?"

"Not yet," said Urgum. "There's a small matter to clear up."

"What?" asked the headnappar.

"One of you trod on Molly's flower bed," said Urgum. "So one of you better say sorry to Molly."

The nappars looked at each other in astonishment and jabbered away in their squeaky voices.

"A flower bed?"

"Out here?"

"Well it wasn't me."

"And definitely not me."

"Or me."

"Where is it?"

"Is that it?"

"Look, somebody's trod in it."

"Well it wasn't me."

"And definitely not me."

"Or me..."

As the chatter got louder and squeakier, Urgum leant back against the rock and sighed. Nappars were so irritating, didn't they realize they were supposed to be fighting? He looked around, expecting to see lots more arriving. *No sign of them yet, but they better hurry up soon,* Urgum thought. As the excited voices got even squeakier, he started running out of patience.

Up in the tree, Molly could hardly bring herself to watch.

She clung to Grizelda's arm for reassurance.

"Seven of them against Dad!" she remarked, trying to sound calm. "It's not fair, we must do something. Shoot some with your bow."

"Are you kidding?" said Grizelda. "Urgum'd be furious if I helped him in a little scrap like this."

"But see how he's looking around! He seems worried."

"Worried? What's he got to worry about?"

"He could be killed!"

"Urgum? Killed?" Grizelda laughed. "Fat chance. Have you ever seen him fight? And I mean *really* fight?"

"Not really."

Grizelda laid herself back along the branch she was sitting on and dangled a long leg lazily down. She ran a hand through her hair and then held a few ends up in front of her face and examined them thoughtfully. It made her go a bit cross-eyed which looked so funny

that for a moment Molly forgot about the danger her father was facing.

"When I was your age," said Grizelda slowly, "I was a slave with the Fat Mutts. Thirty of them tried to raid Golgarth. Urgum, Mungoid and Olk faced them together and beat the lot, but it was mainly Urgum. It's not just his skill or his strength that does it, it's not even that he's totally vicious and merciless. It's his speed. He came out at them so fast that by the time Mungoid and Olk had got organized, all they had to do was mop up the pieces."

"Wow! But still, seven against one isn't fair."

"Too right it isn't fair. Those nappars haven't a chance."

Grizelda looked deep into Molly's worried eyes then sat up to face her properly. When she spoke her voice was softer than Molly had ever heard it.

"Can you keep a secret?" Grizelda asked.

Molly nodded.

"Your father is the most awesome combat fighter I've ever seen. Nobody comes even close. His skill with that axe is something I could only dream of."

Grizelda paused and looked slightly embarrassed. Then in a stern voice she added: "But if you ever tell him I said so, you're dead."

Molly glowed with pride.

Meanwhile, down on the rocks, Urgum couldn't take the noise a moment longer.

"SHUT IT!" he snarled. The squeaky voices fell silent and the nappars turned to him, almost in surprise that he was still there.

"Well?" he said. "I can't be bothered to wait for the others. So is one of you going to say sorry for that

footprint in the flower bed?"

"What others?" said the headnappar.

"Don't change the subject," said Urgum. "Is someone going to shout SORRY MOLLY or have I got to make you?"

The headnapper looked bewildered.

"I don't understand you Urgum," he said. "You are surely about to die, so how come you're still there trying to make it big with us just because of one stupid little flower?"

At first Urgum struggled for an answer, but then he raised his hand to his neck and reached his grubby fingers down the front of his tunic. Very gently he felt around then pulled out what looked like a filthy green string with a few tiny specks of colour clinging to it. It was the flower necklace Molly had given him when he'd first returned from the Unicorn Hunt.

"Didn't you know?" said Urgum. "Stupid little flowers are what all the hard boys are wearing these days."

The headnapper threw back his head and snorted with a contemptuous guffaw, while behind him the other nappars all nudged each other and cackled. Smiling sweetly at them, Urgum tucked the necklace safely back inside his vest then rubbed his shoulder blades comfortably against the rock wall and fingered his axe. The handle felt warm in his hand, every line of the deep wood grain was familiar to him. The weight of the double cutting-head resting on his palm gave him friendly reassurance. He looked around the group of snarling bandits standing elbow to elbow before him. Their hands fumbled into their pockets and belts then several short nappar blades appeared, a couple of spiked clubs and one long thin sword. At last!

Urgum glanced around one last time. No more nappars seemed to be arriving. He took a deep breath and swung his axe up across his chest ready to strike. "Here we go!" He smiled to himself, briefly casting his eyes skywards.

"AM I SCARED?

NO!

DO I CARE?

NO!

I'M COMPLETELY

MENTAL!

Now let's make the gods proud of me."

And at that moment a giant thumb pushed "pause" on the immortal remote control. Without knowing it, Urgum and the nappars froze in time.

A Divine Gamble

Up in the Halls of Sirrus, the twin barbarian gods Tangor and Tangal had settled down to watch their champion in action. It had been a while since Urgum had treated them to a true barbarian spectacle, and they were all set to enjoy it. But just as the nappars were about to move forwards, a third god materialized, seized the remote control and stopped the action.

"Oi!" shouted Tangor. "We were watching that!"

"All ready to see your little fat disciple sliced up are you?" said the stranger.

The twins looked around to see Nappardeus, the god of nappars, who had grabbed the remote control and was holding it out of reach.

"He'll destroy your rabble!" said Tangal.

"Wanna bet?" replied Nappardeus. "Look at him!"

Tangor and Tangal peered closely at Urgum. Behind them Nappardeus sniggered.

"See?" Nappardeus snorted. "He's twitching. He's back against the wall."

"Piffle!" shouted Tangor. "He's going to take all seven of your freaks and wipe the sands with them."

"Nah! He's lost his nerve. Your champion is about to fail."

"Never!" said Tangor.

"We can soon check," said Tangal.

The goddess reached on to a

shelf and pulled down a small wooden box with an open hole across the top. Across the hole were a row of finely stretched hairs and sticking from the end of the box was a highly polished hollow bone. Tangal pointed the bone towards Urgum and the hairs started to vibrate, making a very soft musical note.

"See?" said Tangal. "The nerve detector is registering normal. He's going to thrash your lot."

But then the nerve detector squeaked. Just briefly, but it definitely squeaked.

"Told you!" Nappardeus laughed triumphantly. "He's lost it. He's all show and no go. He'll be minced!"

"No way!" said Tangor.

"Wanna bet?" Nappardeus smirked. "Or are you scared, too?"

"I'm not scared of you!" said Tangor. "But what can we bet with? Being gods we own everything anyway."

"If Urgum wins," said Nappardeus, "I'll kiss your feet."

"Whatever makes you happy," said Tangal. "You nappars are weird."

"But WHEN Urgum loses, you kiss my feet!" Nappardeus laughed. And to show he meant business he stuck his foot up in front of the twin gods' faces.

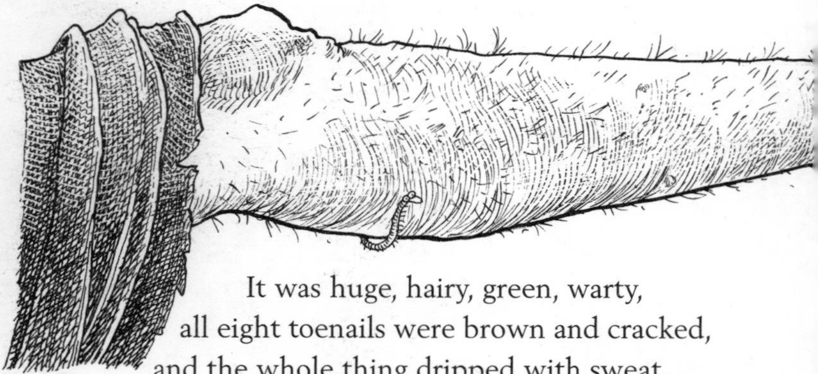

It was huge, hairy, green, warty, all eight toenails were brown and cracked, and the whole thing dripped with sweat.

"Surely that's the most revolting foot in eternity!" Tangal gasped, holding her nose.

"It isn't actually," said Nappardeus. "This is."

Nappardeus showed them his other foot. If the twins hadn't been divine celestial beings, they would have been sick.

"So, are you still backing Urgum?" he said. "Or are you scared too?"

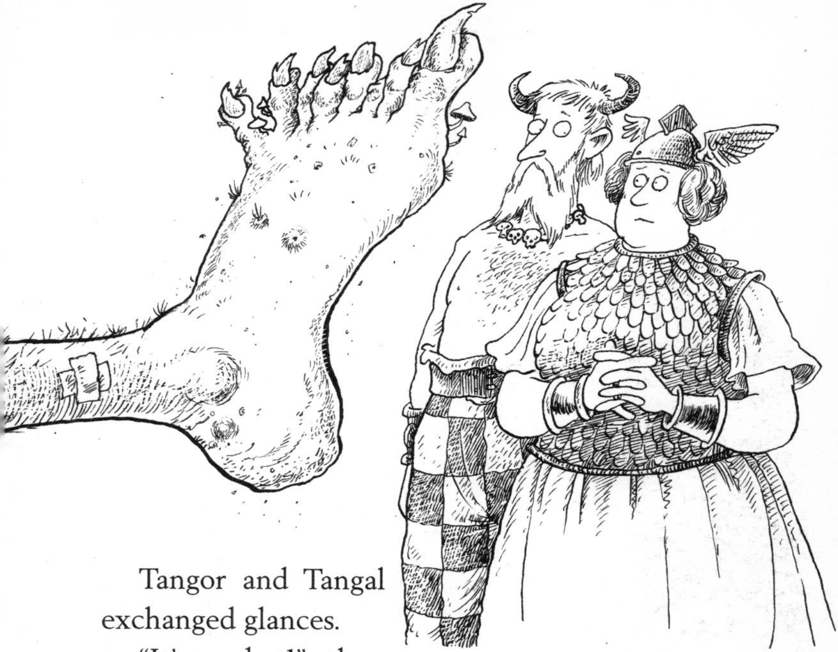

Tangor and Tangal exchanged glances.

"It's a bet!" they said, gritting their teeth.

And so Nappardeus pushed "play" on the remote control...

An Unfair Fight

Back in the world of mortals, the nappars advanced. "I'll tell you a secret, my happy little chappies." Urgum smiled as he casually drummed his fingers on his axe handle. "When there's a pile of oversized vulture-snacks all attacking you together, they can't all get close at once. So all it takes to chop them down is a bit of careful..."

KACHOCKK!

The axe lashed out and a hand fell to the ground. It was still grasping a long thin sword. But Urgum had no time to admire it, because a second nappar was lunging forward on his other side...

SHPLUTT!

Urgum shoved the end of the axe handle straight up into the leering nappar's face. As it staggered backwards a crunching blow from a nailed club ripped into Urgum's right shoulder, but already the axe head had swung upwards...

BLETCHH!

The jaw of the clubber cracked open showering Urgum with bloody teeth...

CLONG!

With a side swipe the axe head smacked into the face of the next nappar, sending him flying over the fallen swordsman. Ignoring the blood pouring from his shoulder, Urgum stepped forward. (An old combat trick: step away from the wall and immediately there'll be one coward who will try and come in from behind you).

Without looking round, Urgum leapt into the air with his legs apart and swung the axe round underneath himself.

KUR-RUTCH!

The nappar behind him was almost split into two pieces from the bottom upwards. Urgum dropped to one knee, ripped out the axe and brought it round in an arc...

FPLOPP!

He buried it deep into the gut of yet another lumbering nappar.

That left only the headnappar himself who was standing back, aghast, his sword trembling in his hand. Urgum caught his breath and the axe finally came to a halt. The whole operation had taken less time than a leaf falling from a tree. Around him the nappers writhed and moaned as they tried to drag each other away from the fiercest savage the Lost Desert had ever known.

"As I was saying," Urgum continued, "all it takes is a bit of careful *timing*. So are you going to say sorry, or wait for the others?"

"Others?" said the headnappar. "What others?"

"There's supposed to be seven of you."

"That's all of us," said the headnappar. "Six bleeding on the ground and me."

"Don't you lie to me!" shouted Urgum.

Diving forward and swinging the axe at arm's length, he caught the headnappar's legs and brought him crashing down to the ground. With a leap, Urgum was over him and the axe was ready to strike. Grizelda and Molly had already scrambled down from the tree and were running towards him.

"Well?" demanded Urgum. "Here comes Molly, so this is your last chance. Say sorry!"

"SORRY MOLLY!" screamed the headnappar. "SORRY FOR STANDING ON YOUR FLOWER BED. I'M SO SORRY. SORRY SORRY SORRY."

"That's OK," said Molly, shrugging her shoulders. "I'm sure it was an accident. Forget it."

Urgum lowered his axe and stood back. Taking his chance, the headnappar scrambled away followed by the others, leaving long dark trails of blood behind them. Urgum, Molly and Grizelda watched as they disappeared into the distant desert, with Djinta and Percy patiently following them high above. The coward who had crept behind Urgum was making especially slow and painful progress. Overhead, the vultures licked their beaks. The first course of their dinner was almost ready.

"There Molly," said Urgum. "At least you got your apology."

"But look at your shoulder, Dad!" said Molly. "Does it hurt?"

"Well of course it hurts." Urgum flexed his arm. "No point being brave if things like this don't hurt. But come on, let's get home before the others arrive."

"What others?" asked Molly and Grizelda together.

"You know," said Urgum. "The others! You said there were seven of them. The rest will be here soon."

"Dad!" Molly sighed. "That was the lot, that was all seven of them."

"Don't lie to your father! I know what seven is. Seven men covers a hillside. I fought seven before, the army of Magoon."

"Urgum," said Grizelda, "that was seven *hundred*."

"Is that different?" asked Urgum.

"Very different," said Grizelda.

"No wonder you looked worried!" Molly chuckled.

"ME? WORRIED?" Urgum bellowed. But then he relaxed and sighed. "Well, maybe a tiny bit, but it wasn't my fault. I blame all this fancy mathematics."

Urgum let the axe fall from his grasp and clutched his shoulder. Blood oozed between his fingers. Grizelda ripped a clean piece of sleeve from her own shirt, folded it into a pad and pressed it to Urgum's wound.

Up in the Halls of Sirrus the twin gods were celebrating.

"Urgum Urgum!" cheered Tangal. "He was ready to take on seven hundred nappars!"

"Hey, Nappardeus!" called out Tangor, sticking up his foot. "Come here and get kissing."

But Nappardeus wasn't giving up that easily. He decided to take matters into his own hands. Actually, he decided to take matters into somebody else's hand. He dematerialized and transmitted himself down to the hand that lay on the ground still clutching the long pointed sword. After checking that Urgum and Grizelda were several paces away, with their backs towards him, Nappardeus made the hand rise slowly from the ground, its blade pointed towards Urgum's heart. He carefully took aim, but he had overlooked one important detail.

Molly had gone back to stand where Urgum had been, imagining what it must have been like to take on seven giant nappars. To her amazement she saw the hand holding the sword quietly rise up beside her. She watched fascinated as it steadied itself but when she realized it was taking aim at her father, Molly's natural instinct took over. Faster than she could cry out, she raised her spade and cracked it down on the fingers as hard as she could. The sword flew free, and in one swift movement Molly caught it and plunged it straight through the palm of the hand.

Nappardeus looked up to the clouds. He could hear great guffaws of divine laughter. Obviously other gods had joined the twins to watch.

"Look everybody!" Tangor said. "The nappar god got beaten by a little girl!"

"No wonder." Tangal laughed. "He might be a god, but he's still just a nappar and she's a barbarian."

Nappardeus hung his head and dematerialized. All in all, it hadn't been a good day for the most irritating tribe in the Lost Desert.

"Come on, Urgum," Grizelda was saying. "You better get back to my place and I'll patch you up properly. Molly, can you give us a hand?"

"Certainly!" Molly ran up with the sword, showing off her bloody trophy. The fingers were still twitching. "How about this one?"

Grizelda laughed.

Urgum gave her a hug. "That's my girl!" he said.

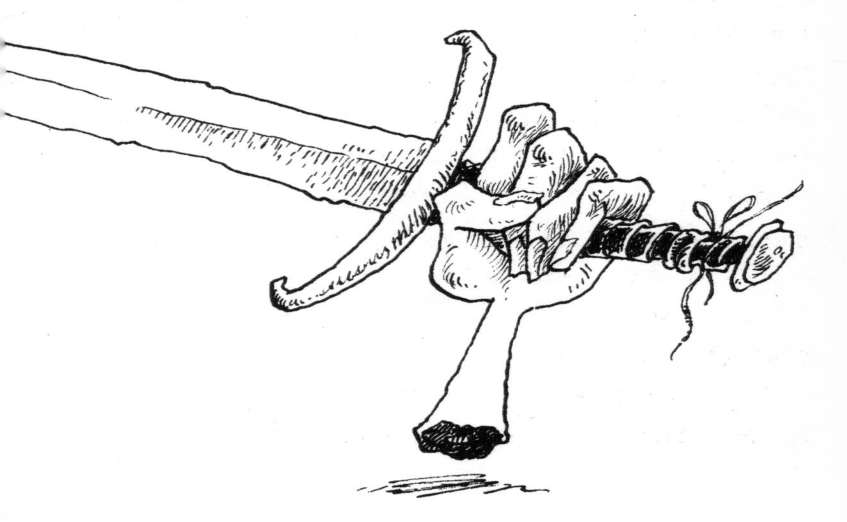

Too Many Little Secrets

Olk was still wearing his joke green hair bandage as they passed him, and Urgum had been right. Molly did think it was funny. In fact she thought it was so funny that not only did Olk forget to ask for the password, he was so desperate to think of another equally totally hilarious joke that he completely forgot to move or speak for the next six weeks.

On the steps outside Grizelda's, Molly was holding the dripping bit of ripped sleeve to Urgum's wound. Grizelda had gone in to boil up some healing potion, and Divina had come across to find out what had happened.

"You should have seen Dad, Mum," said Molly.

"Oh, I've seen him," said Divina sternly. "And I dare say I'll see him again."

"But Mum, he was just so cool!" Molly insisted.

"It doesn't strike me as very cool getting a lump hacked out of your arm," remarked Divina, examining Urgum's wound.

"Oh come on!" said Molly. "The way he faced those seven nappars, especially when he thought it was going to be seven hundred."

"That sounds rather silly if you ask me," said Divina. "Oh well, I suppose I'd better find a clean bandage."

Divina set off back to their cave, not letting them see her proud grin. Molly carefully peeled the cloth away from the wound and was glad to see that the worst of the bleeding had stopped.

"Well, I thought you were cool," she said.

"Oh, it was nothing," said Urgum. "Especially with you and Grizelda to back me up."

"What could we have done?" asked Molly.

"Haven't you seen Grizelda with her bow and arrows?"

"I thought you didn't like them."

"Baby toys," agreed Urgum. "But somehow she works

magic with them. I never even saw the arrow that hit that first nappar, he was so far away from both of us. But you think about it – if she'd only scratched him, he'd have run off and taken you with him. If she'd killed him straight out, you might have fallen head first to the rocks. And if she'd hit you ... well anyway it was one amazing shot to bring him down slowly like that."

Urgum glanced back at Grizelda's cave entrance, then leant over to Molly and whispered urgently, "Can you keep a secret?"

Molly nodded.

"I tell you, Grizelda is the most awesome archer I've ever seen. There's nobody comes even close. Her skill with those arrows is something I could only dream of." Urgum sighed. "But if you tell her I said so, you're dead."

To his astonishment, Molly burst out laughing.

Just then a familiar figure came riding into the basin on his ox.

"It's Mungoid!" said Molly, running over to meet him. "Where have you been you lovely big ugly thing?"

"Shhh!" said Mungoid, getting down from the sweating beast. "Can you keep a secret?"

Molly nodded. She was getting to be an expert at secrets.

Mungoid beckoned Molly round to the far side of the ox in case Urgum looked over and saw what he was doing. He opened his knapbag and carefully took out a small parcel wrapped in silk which he passed to Molly.

"It's for you," he said sheepishly. "I just got it at the market."

Molly carefully unwrapped it, and there was a little pot containing a perfect purple sandrose.

"Aw! Thanks Mungoid." Molly smiled. "It's a real beauty, but what's it for?"

"To say sorry for me standing on the last one."

Molly gasped. "So after all that, it was you!"

"And don't you dare tell Urgum I've been buying little flowers," said Mungoid. "Or you're dead."

"Right," said Molly. She was just about to hurry to the cave to hide her present when a cheeky thought crossed her mind.

"I tell you something, Mungoid," she whispered. "I never thought you'd be giving me a sandrose when there's Grizelda available."

"But ... but why would I want to ... to give Grizelda..." Mungoid's voice tailed off, then he stared down at the ground and kicked one of his huge feet with the other. "Yeah, well, I'm working on it," he said. "But that's another secret and if you tell anybody then you're double dead!"

"Good for you Mungoid." Molly smiled, giving his arm a friendly squeeze before dashing away.

Once the sandrose was safely hidden in her room, Molly came out and bumped into Divina who was in the lounge, bending over a deep wooden chest and rummaging around for something to use as a bandage.

"Honestly, Mum," said Molly crossly to her back. "You could be a bit nicer to Dad. He probably saved my life back there."

Her mother looked up then smiled shyly.

"Can you keep a secret?" asked Divina.

Molly did a little careful nod because all these secrets were starting to make her head heavy.

"He definitely saved your life back there," said Divina, burying her head back in the box. "And that's why he's not just cool, but the coolest dad in the whole desert."

"Then why couldn't you say so?" demanded Molly.

"Well..." said Divina without looking up again, "if he truly knew what I thought of him then he'd be so smug that I'd just have to kill him or something."

Divina tugged a neat white cloth from the chest, then straightened up and gave Molly a very serious look.

"So that's why I never really tell him what I think of him and that's why you won't tell him either," she said matter-of-factly.

By the time Molly and Divina had got back over to Urgum, Grizelda was sitting next to him. The large-eyed meebobs had carried out a steaming cauldron of healing potion and, having safely put it down, they hurried back into the darkness again. Mungoid had tied up his ox and was heading towards them and Molly noticed that his three hairs had been smoothed down.

"That shoulder looks pretty," called out Mungoid. "So what's it all about? Been having fun?"

"Some nappars trod on Molly's flower bed and they wouldn't apologize," said Urgum.

"Ooops!" Mungoid tried not to blush. "I mean, oh really? Gosh aren't nappars just the pits? Hope it doesn't hurt too much."

"Yee-owwww!" shouted Urgum as Grizelda sloshed some boiling health potion on his shoulder.

"Stop yowking, you big baby," said Grizelda as the blue steam rose into the air. "Honestly, if only you didn't rely on that stupid old axe of yours..."

"Well if you were more use with your silly pingy arrows..."

"At least she wasn't silly enough to get herself chopped up." Divina wrapped the bandage around his arm, jerking it slightly tighter than was absolutely necessary.

"I blame the nappar that trod on the flower bed myself," said Mungoid.

Molly had heard enough.

"Hey, all of you!" she announced. "One of you told

me a secret today. Who'd like to hear it?"

"Don't you dare!" said Urgum, Grizelda, Divina and Mungoid all together. *Twink plink dink,* Mungoid's three hairs shot up again.

Then they turned and looked at each other suspiciously.

Then they all turned and looked at Molly again.

"Only kidding!" she said, and collapsed in a fit of laughter.

PART FOUR
The TAX WARS
LAPLACE PALACE

An official visit

Early one morning, Molly was sitting on her bed in her room carefully counting her secret hoard of coins even though she knew exactly how many there were. One, two, three, four, five, six ... seven bronze tannas. If she got eleven more she'd have eighteen which was halfway to a silver tanna! Molly was so excited by this thought that she decided to count them again when...

"ARGHHHHHH!"

Urgum's scream had come from the room next door. Molly hurriedly bundled the coins up into the velvet

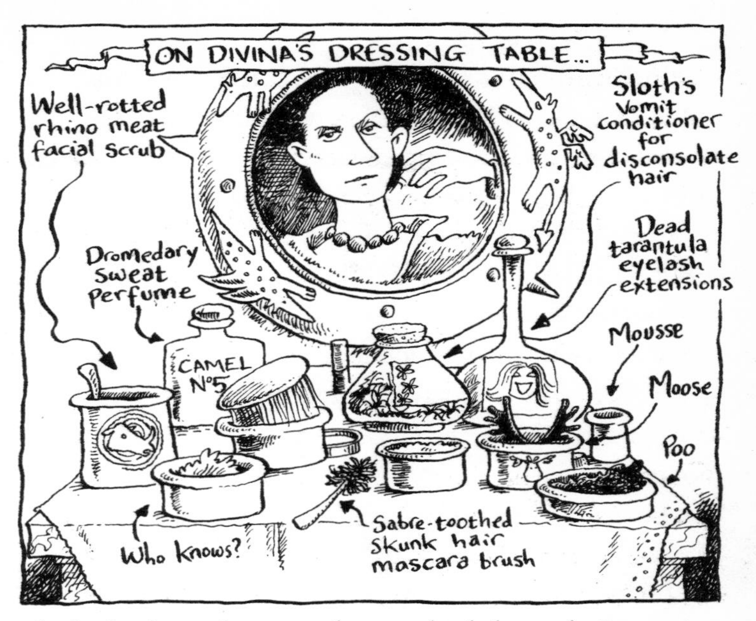

cloth she kept them in, then rushed through. It was just as she expected. Urgum was sitting on the floor holding his foot to his mouth and sucking his big toe. Lying beside him was his big axe. Divina was sitting at her dressing table doing her hair, ignoring him.

"Have you just banged your big toe on your axe and chopped it down the middle again?" Molly asked.

"Umm umma oom." Urgum nodded.

"Serves you right for leaving it lying around," Divina sniffed.

Urgum gave his split toe a final lick then stuck his red tongue out at Divina. Even without speaking, it was obvious that he was saying, "Since you did the place up, there's nowhere for it to go."

In reply Divina raised her eyebrow which silently shouted at him, "Don't go blaming me if every night you just throw that dirty great axe down on the floor by the bed and then forget about it."

"Well if you two have quite finished arguing," said Molly, using real words, "I'm going back to counting my money."

"Counting money?" muttered Urgum. "What a waste of time."

"But I could have a silver tanna soon!" said Molly as she made a few marks on the dirt floor with a stick. A couple more strokes and a squiggle and she'd finished her calculation. "I just need twenty-nine more bronze ones."

"Don't start getting into all that." Urgum got to his feet and hobbled over to sit on the bed. "Money's just a numbers thing for making softhands happy. If they have a bigger number of money than somebody else then they think that makes them better. All this fancy mathematics only leads to trouble."

"But I thought you liked trouble?" said Molly.

"I do," agreed Urgum as he pulled his boots on. "But I like real trouble, not just who's got the biggest number trouble."

"But if I've got money, I could buy you a present." Molly pointed at her little bundle of coins. "What would you like?"

"A great big fight." Urgum grinned.

"Oh dear," said Molly. "I don't know if money can buy that."

Urgum sighed."It's like I've always said. What's the point of money if it can't buy you what you want?"

But just then Molly thought of something that Urgum *did* want. It only cost five tannas too, so she slipped the little bundle of coins into her pocket all ready for next time the hawkers came calling.

GOYY-ANGGGG!

A massive sound barged into the cave, clumsily bounced its way down to the back, turned left at the archways, staggered along the corridor and blundered into the bedroom where it hit the ceiling and shook a spider down on to Urgum's head.

"It's the door chime!" Divina threw down her hairbrush and nimbly nipped out to the cave entrance, adjusting her earrings as she went.

"I wish she wouldn't call it that," remarked Urgum as he and Molly followed her out to the front of the cave. "It makes it sound so tinny."

Sure enough, Olk the sentry had smashed his elephant-stunning mallet into the giant gong that hung beside him in the mouthway of the rock basin. As the vibrations died away, feathers fluttered down from the startled vultures overhead, while under the ground the skeletons of long-dead warriors rattled.

The boys were sitting outside the front of the cave idly lobbing scorpions at each other. On hearing the gong, Ruinn had wandered across the basin to look out and see who was there.

"Just some posh woman on a horse," he announced as he returned. "From the palace."

"The palace?" Divina gasped. "Honestly! They might have warned us."

She disappeared back into the bedroom to make herself even more presentable.

"Funny looking she is," said Ruinn, plonking himself back down on the ground beside the others. "Not a savage, and definitely not a softhand."

Urgum peered out of the cave entrance and across to the mouthway of the basin. When he saw the visitor waiting on the other side of Olk, a big smile came to his face. She had perfect straight white hair and was wearing the long green and gold robes of the Laplace Palace, but her unnaturally large eyes, elongated back and shortened legs betrayed the fact that this was no ordinary female.

"Wow!" he remarked. "They've sent a dizzalid!"

"What's that then?" asked Molly.

"Half woman, half lizard," replied Urgum approvingly. "And as tough as they come. I wonder what she's all about then?"

By now all the boys had turned to look towards the main entrance. The dizzalid wasn't wearing the armoured hat of the Laplace guards, and she didn't have the badge of the estate managers either. What she did have was a big dull-looking book tucked under her left arm.

"Password?" boomed Olk, but the dizzalid was not impressed.

"I ask the questions," she said in a low authoritative voice.

Taking the book in her thick fingers, she opened it and riffled through a few pages covered in dense scribbles. Finally, she ran a finger-claw down a list of names and then called out "Urgum, son of Urgurt, come forth." She sat back comfortably in her saddle,

obviously expecting to be obeyed instantly.

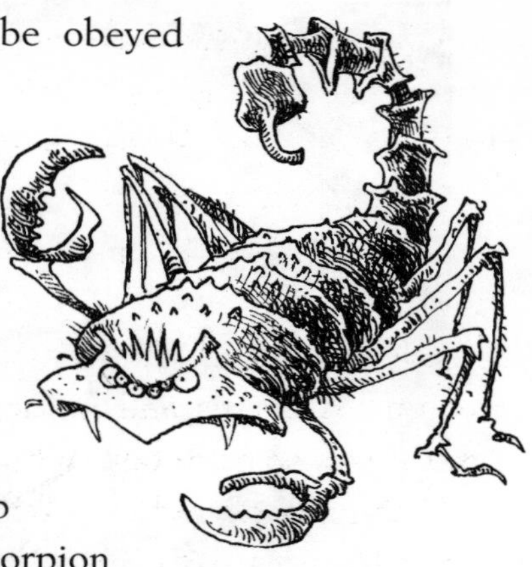

"Hey Dad, she wants to see you," said Ruff.

"Well I'm a bit busy at the moment," said Urgum, which was true. Rakk and Rekk had just managed to lob a particularly lively scorpion down the back of his neck and Urgum was hopping about trying to catch it with one hand shoved down the top of his vest and the other shoved up from underneath.

"What does she want anyway?" he asked. His contortions were making him go red-faced as Rakk and Rekk fell about with laughter.

"How should I know?" said Ruff.

"Well go and ASK her!" said Urgum.

With a bored teenage mutter, Ruff rose to his feet and slouched towards the mouthway. He hadn't intended to step out past Olk, but his interest in the curious person on the horse got the better of him. As he emerged from the cragg wall and approached, one of the dizzalid's huge eyes swivelled round to watch him with a cold stare. The other eye couldn't be bothered.

"What do you want?" he demanded.

"Are you Urgum son of Urgurt?" she asked in her low voice.

"No," said Ruff. This female lizard thing had already got on his nerves and he decided he'd make a point. "But if you want to talk to him, first you talk to me."

"I think not," said the dizzalid curtly. "I want Urgum son of Urgurt here. Fetch him."

"Well actually he's a bit busy right now," said Ruff. "So why don't you get lost?"

WHALLUMP - GADOYYING!

Ruff had no idea where the big green thing that slammed into his chest came from, but whatever it was, it lifted him right off his feet and smashed him head first into Olk's gong.

"Nice one!" The boys all cheered. They had gathered on the safe side of Olk to watch their oldest brother making an idiot of himself.

The dizzalid casually tucked her massive tail back under her robes, then she pushed her hair back with a flick of her black-forked tongue and stared at them.

"I am waiting for Urgum, son of Urgurt," she repeated, tapping her stumpy fingers on the book. "And in the meantime, who is this?"

She was looking at Olk as if she had only just realized he was there. The muscles across the sentry's massive back stiffened and the tip of the great blade that was slung over his shoulder started to quiver.

"That's Olk!" said Rekk and Rakk eagerly. All the boys hurriedly stepped back a few paces in case that blade should suddenly sweep around, but the dizzalid didn't so much as twitch.

"Olk," she repeated thoughtfully. While one eye still surveyed the sentry, the other looked down at the page of her book. "Olk of Golgarth ... yes, here he is. Income zero. We're not going to get much out of you then, are we? So relax, big boy, you've nothing to worry about."

A low gurgle echoed deep inside Olk's great gut and

the end of the blade drooped slightly and went still. The boys gasped! Was it their imagination or had Olk really relaxed?

"Thank you," mumbled the giant sentry.

"Keep your thanks," said the dizzalid. "Our purpose is to be fair. We only take what's due to us."

Now the boys really were buzzing. They had actually heard Olk say "thank you"! Who *was* this strange official? They simply had to know.

"Dad!" they shouted. "Get over here, you're wanted. NOW!"

At this point the immaculate-looking Divina stepped from the cave and was just getting terribly excited about presenting herself to the person from the palace when she saw Urgum lying on the ground bouncing himself along on his back.

"And exactly WHAT are you doing?" she demanded.

"There's a scorpion down my vest and I'm trying to squash it," said Urgum.

"There's no time for that now, you big baby," snapped Divina, hoisting him to his feet. "We've got a visitor!"

"Eeek!" squealed Urgum. "I think it slipped down into my trousers."

* * *

Urgum started to undo his belt but Divina slapped his hands away from his buckle. Quickly she scooped the dirt out of his ears and wiped a blob of gravy off his chin.

"Gerroff!" moaned Urgum.

"She's from the *palace*!" hissed Divina. "And just for once it would be nice if we could make a good impression, so don't you dare let me down."

Walking very carefully, so as not to disturb his eight-legged twin-pincered poison-tailed intruder, Urgum stepped out past Olk and eyed up the stern-looking woman sitting on her horse. Even though he had a big respect for dizzalids, Urgum didn't like palace officials much so he decided to pull a really tough mean face. This looked a bit strange because next to him Divina was smiling ever so graciously, being the perfect hostess.

"I am Urgum, son of Urgurt," he growled. "So who are you?"

"I am the chief inspector from the Laplace Palace department of taxation," said the dizzalid.

"And...?" said Urgum trying to ignore the nasty itchy feeling he was getting crawling around just below the belt.

"Our records show that your household is earning an income."

"I've never made any income in my life," declared Urgum proudly. "I just eat and sleep and fight and occasionally sing rude songs very loudly to annoy my wife."

Divina tried to force a jolly laugh.

"Oh, my husband can be such a tease." She giggled desperately. "You really mustn't believe a word he says."

"I don't," said the dizzalid curtly. One eye flickered between Divina and Urgum, the other gazed down into the book. "According to our records, we have a claim from Suprema, the chancellor's wife, who once bought some flowered necklaces from you."

"Do I look like I sell flowered necklaces?" bellowed Urgum.

This suggestion had sent him into such a rage that he started stomping around crossly. He had completely forgotten about his little visitor who was getting a bit scared of being bumped around in the dark and was preparing its poisoned tail to strike.

"I'll have you know," cried Urgum, "that I'm the fiercest savage that the Lost Desert has ever ...

YOWWW YEEEK YAH!"

The little visitor had struck. Urgum hopped away beating the back of his trousers with his hands as hard as he could, trying to squash the scorpion before it stung him again.

"I'm so sorry about him," said Divina who was blushing with embarrassment.

The dizzalid was amazed. One eye followed Urgum while the other looked straight at Divina.

"I've seen people make all sorts of sad and pathetic excuses for not paying their taxes," said the dizzalid. "But I must admit, that's the first time I've ever seen anyone run around smacking their own bottom."

"Oh he's such a hoot." Divina tried desperately to look amused as Urgum reached the cragg wall and started frantically rubbing his bottom up and down against it. "My Urgum's always doing funny little things to amuse us."

"Such as making flower jewellery?" asked the dizzalid dryly.

"Oh no!" said Divina. "That's my daughter Molly. You must meet her. MOLLY!"

Molly had been waiting behind Olk with the boys, but on hearing her name she skipped out to join Divina and the strange-looking lady from the palace.

"This is Molly, my daughter," said Divina proudly. "She's ever so clever with her flowers and things."

"And then she sells them," said the dizzalid.

"That's right," said Molly, taking the folded cloth from her pocket and unwrapping it to show the coins. "So far I've made seven bronze tannas altogether."

Just for once the dizzalid's eyes both looked the same way – at Molly's little coins. The black tongue flickered around the lips hungrily, then one of the eyes went back to check the book.

"Is that all?" muttered the dizzalid, obviously thinking her trip hadn't been worth the trouble. "Oh well, you're on the official records now so welcome to the system."

"What does that mean?" asked Molly.

"Hasn't your mother explained to you about the workings of civilized society?" asked the dizzalid.

"Oh indeed I have," gushed Divina. "And she's fascinated by it all, aren't you Molly?"

Molly smiled weakly, wondering if her mother had gone mad.

"So you will understand that those tannas count as income," said the dizzalid who was still staring at Molly's coins. "Therefore you are liable to pay half of them in tax."

"Tax?" asked Molly. "What's that?"

"Oh dear," muttered Divina, feeling awkward. Although she had told Molly about some of the aspects of civilized society such as the solid ruby palace and the exquisite food and satin cushions the size of elephants, there were other bits she hadn't quite got round to mentioning. Tax was one of them.

"Half of all cash earnings must be rendered to the State," explained the dizzalid.

"HA HA HA!" the boys laughed, behind Olk.

"What for?" demanded Molly.

"It's to pay for public services, dear," explained Divina gently.

"So what's that then?" asked Molly looking round blankly. There wasn't much evidence of any public services at Golgarth.

"If we didn't have public services, we couldn't have a palace or a princess," explained Divina.

"But Mum, we haven't got a palace or princess!" exclaimed Molly. "We've got a cave and a bunch of smelly brothers."

"Er, but ... ah!" said Divina, desperately trying to think why tax was so marvellous. "Tax pays for all sorts of important people who we never see but they do vital work such as ... well, they make lists of other people's names..."

"Oh yeah?" said Molly, unimpressed.

"Oh yes," said Divina hurriedly. "And then there's other people who check the lists and then some more people are needed to count the lists to make sure they've got enough lists..."

Urgum laughed "...but mainly, tax pays for tax collectors!"

Molly turned to see her father walking back towards them, rubbing his bottom and clutching a dead scorpion between his finger and thumb.

"I did try to warn you about money, Molly!" He grinned. "It just brings trouble."

Molly looked sadly at the seven little coins in her hand. "So I've got to give half of my money away, have I?" she asked. "But you can't do half of seven."

"I can," said the dizzalid. "You owe three and a half bronze tannas."

"Is that right, Dad?" asked Molly crossly.

"Ask your mother," said Urgum. "She's the civilized one."

Divina gulped. As a softhand child she had always had everything she had ever wanted, but had never wondered or even cared where the money to pay for it all came from. Now she knew and she felt rotten.

"Have I really got to pay?" said Molly.

Divina nodded sadly, and felt even more guilty when Molly simply shrugged her shoulders and held out her hard-earnt coins towards the dizzalid.

"I'm not supposed to take it." The dizzalid sniffed. "We have a collection department for that."

"First inspectors, then collectors," said Urgum. "No wonder tax is so expensive. Why can't you just take it and save the collectors a trip?"

"I suppose I could," said the dizzalid.

"How can you take three and a half anyway?" asked Molly.

"I can't," said the dizzalid. "So I take four. That way, the debt is cleared."

Molly counted out four of the little coins and passed them up to the dizzalid's thick-fingered hand. The dizzalid dropped them into a small pouch on her belt, then took a small leadstick and made a mark in her book. Molly was left holding just three bronze tannas.

"Hang on," said Urgum. "Even I can see that you took more coins than she's got left."

"She will be credited," said the dizzalid writing in her book. "Half of one bronze tanna ... to Molly of Golgarth. There, you're on the records now so from time to time the collectors will be passing and you'll know what to do."

Divina was trying to be the perfect hostess and say things like "Thank you for dropping in" and "Do call again" but it all seemed so unfair that she was lost for words. To her amazement it was Urgum who performed the social niceties.

"Here." He held up the dead scorpion in front of the dizzalid. "You want this?"

The dizzalid's eyes opened wide and for a moment she almost seemed to smile.

"Catch," said Urgum tossing the scorpion up towards her.

The dizzalid's black tongue shot out, caught the scorpion in mid-air and flicked it into her mouth. With a crunch and a swallow it was gone.

"Thank you," she said, looking surprised. "That was a very kind thought. I had no idea that a savage could be so, well ... er, civilized."

"Oh we're dead posh we are, aren't we dear?" said Urgum nudging Divina who couldn't answer. The smile on her face had frozen so solid in shock that she looked like she was trying to bite an invisible plate in half.

As the dizzalid rode away down Smiley Alley, the boys and Molly were all jamming their fingers in their ears and clenching their eyes tight shut. They suspected that this was going to be a very loud one, and they were extremely correct.

"URGUMMMMMMM!" screamed Divina at last. Even Olk's gong was jealous. It couldn't make a noise as damaging as that.

"Yes dear," he replied quietly, trying not to snigger.

"How ... how could you?" she cried. "She's from the PALACE. And you gave her a DEAD SCORPION to EAT!"

"It takes all sorts to fill this desert," explained Urgum. "And we've all got different tastes. It so happens that scorpions are a dizzalid's favourite food. Didn't you see her bolt it down?"

Divina took a deep breath then thought about this.

"True," she admitted and gradually began to relax. After a moment she even smiled, and this time it wasn't one of those "How-lovely-to-see-you-because-you're-from-the-palace" smiles. It was a proper big-eyed smile, the sort that made Urgum feel all warm and a bit giggly.

"Thank you Urgie," she said, stroking his arm with her finger. "I'm sure we've made a good impression on her after all."

Looking happy and contented, Divina stepped past Olk and all the boys (who didn't see or hear her because they still had their eyes and ears shut) and headed towards the cave. Urgum was about to follow but Molly pulled him back.

"Dad?" she asked suspiciously. "Were you really being nice to that lizard woman?"

"Nice?" Urgum laughed. "Did you honestly think your old dad was going to be nice to somebody who had just pinched some of his little girl's precious tannas?"

"But you gave her that scorpion!" declared Molly. "And you said it was her favourite food."

"True," said Urgum, "but what's your favourite food, Molly?"

"Probably burnt duck wings," said Molly.

"But how would you like burnt duck wings if you knew that they'd been stewing down the back of my trousers most of the afternoon?"

"Oh that's totally vommo!" Molly spat in disgust.

"So let's just hope your mother never realizes where I got that scorpion from," said Urgum.

Molly burst out laughing so much that it was almost worth four bronze tannas.

Satisfied Customers

Molly only had three tannas left but she needed five to buy the present she wanted for her father. So, in the days that followed, she tried to sell some more of her flower jewellery. Every morning, she wandered down Smiley Alley to sit by the crossroads beside the huge old Sacrifice Tree with her pieces laid out on a cloth in front of her but, unfortunately, every day was the same. Occasionally a few savages would ride past, but on seeing her they would spur on their horses and hurry past in case anybody caught them looking at a few flowers. Molly got more and more bored, and with nothing better to do she spent most of her time lobbing

stones at
the milligobs
that were feeding on the dried
bits of flesh that still clung to
the skeletons chained to the
tree. The bigger milligobs
also tended to eat the
smaller milligobs,
and the very
biggest
ended up
looking like sloppy white balloons covered in tiny wriggly legs and hundreds of little pink mouths with black pin-sized teeth. Molly found it hard to imagine that anything could look more revolting until she discovered that a well aimed rock could burst them open and make all their thin blue veins explode everywhere. But even this stopped being funny after a while.

The only other thing of any interest at all in the area was a plant which was growing a short distance away. On the first day it looked just like a small grey cactus, but by the next morning Molly noticed that it was the height of a man. She couldn't resist walking over for a better look, but when she approached, it started shaking and making an excited hissing sound so she decided to keep well away. A couple of days later, the plant had blossomed out into a fully developed Giant Juppotan, a man-eating cactus with a massive jaw cunningly disguised to look like the entrance to a restaurant. Growing down the back of the plant was a panel of stiff membranes which vibrated in the soft desert breeze making the exact sound of a party of people enjoying a drink and a meal and singing along to a live harp and bongo band. But for all its efforts, the plant wasn't having any more luck than Molly was.

Then, one afternoon, just as Molly was about to give up, she saw a flame-haired female galloping up from the distance and her hopes raised slightly. It was Grizelda the Grisly! Sometimes Grizelda had money, so maybe she would show a bit of interest in buying something?

"Hi Grizelda!" she called, and to her delight the armour clad female savage pulled her horse to a halt.

"Hello Molly," said Grizelda, but her eyes were turned towards the mysterious restaurant entrance. From inside came the sounds of people laughing and the smell of pineapple and porcupine pizza. "Pah! Just my

RESTAURANT
EATS

luck. A new place opens and I haven't got any money."

"No money?" Molly gasped.

"Hey, you couldn't lend me a few tannas could you?" said Grizelda leaping down from her horse. She was still peering towards the inviting doorway, and by now the smell drifting from it had mutated into the rich waft of strawberry and orchid ice cream. Although Grizelda was feared throughout the Lost Desert as a ruthless and deadly assassin, there was still a bit of gurlie inside her that turned into bubbles at the thought of a tall goblet full of calorie-packed pudding.

"If I had any spare tannas I wouldn't be sitting here," said Molly. "I need two more to get a present for Dad."

"Oh yeah," said Grizelda. "I forgot about that. Too bad. Still, watch my horse will you? I'll just have a look inside anyway."

And before Molly could stop her, Grizelda had slipped off her helmet, smoothed her hair back and with a gleam in her eye she was walking up to the restaurant door, unaware that it was opening wider and starting to drip with thick saliva.

"GRIZELDA!" shouted Molly. "NO!"

But Molly's voice was drowned out by a sudden burst of cheering and applause from the restaurant. Quickly

Molly dived towards the Sacrifice Tree and grabbing the largest of the milligobs she hurled it with all her might. It flew right over Grizelda's head and in through the opening where it landed on the floor and burst open.

SHQUEELCH!

A curtain of gluey saliva fell across the doorway, which then quickly collapsed down to the size of a rat's belly button right in front of Grizelda.

"Oh yulchy yukkoid!" said Grizelda. She hurriedly stepped away but a few strands of the rubbery saliva had caught her boot, and she fell backwards to the ground. Pulling out her hand-dagger she scraped herself free of the sticky green mess and then shuffled backwards all the way over to Molly.

"Are you OK?" asked Molly.

Grizelda shook her head, blinked several times and then looked up at the plant. Slowly the restaurant door was opening up and taking shape again. The fat milligob hadn't lasted long. Grizelda shuddered and took a few deep breaths.

"I owe you big time, Molly!" she said at last.

"Thanks," said Molly. "But two tannas will do."

"Sorry," said Grizelda. "I can't help there."

Just then they saw a horse-drawn carriage approaching down the path.

"Softhands!" said Molly. "They've always got money!"

"Looks like your luck might be changing after all!" said Grizelda.

"I hope so," said Molly. "You better go now."

"Why?"

"I don't want you scaring them away!" said Molly.

"If you're sure..."

"Go on! See you back at the cragg."

Grizelda pulled her helmet back on, and then, after wishing Molly good luck, she leapt on to her horse and cantered off down Smiley Alley. Molly arranged her best pieces and then stood neatly beside them with her hands clasped politely in front of her and waited for the carriage to approach. On it she could see an old softhand lady and gentleman wearing the purple robes of the pensioned class.

These were the people who had finished doing jobs which were paid for by the taxes of the workers, and now did nothing, which was also paid for by the taxes of the workers.

"Please stop!" thought Molly, and to her delight they did stop, but unfortunately it was not for her.

"Look at this new place!" said the old gentleman, looking at the restaurant doorway. "And I say, is that a rather natty harp and bongo band I hear playing?"

"You're far too old to be whooping it up with harp and bongo bands." The old lady chuckled. "Mmm, but is that roasted turtle I can smell?"

"Don't go in there!" said Molly. "It's a plant."

"Ugh!" said the lady, looking down and noticing her for the first time. "It's a little savage."

"If you bite the horses I'll have you whipped," the old man said to Molly.

"No, please don't do that!" said Molly, trying to keep her temper. If she hadn't wanted their money so badly she'd have happily let them go and whoop it up with the milligob in the restaurant. Instead she took a deep breath and smiled her nicest smile. "I was just wondering if you'd like to buy some of my flower jewels? Only two bronze tannas."

"Certainly not," said the lady. "They've probably got bugs and nasties on them."

"Absolutely!" said the old man, but then he suddenly seemed distracted by something he saw over Molly's head. "Oh, er, ah ... but don't you think that flower bracelet looks rather nice?"

"What?" The lady gasped in disgust. "How can a bracelet be nice without diamonds? I'd rather die than touch it!"

"Have a closer look!" insisted the old man, nodding earnestly. As Molly bent down to pick up the flower bracelet, the man nudged his wife and pointed at what he had seen.

"Are you sure you'd rather die?" he hissed.

"Oh!" said the lady, rather startled. "Ah yes, well, no, but of course not..."

Molly passed the flower bracelet up for them to inspect.

"It is very truly lovely," said the man. "How much can I pay you for this?"

"Two bronze tannas, sir," said Molly trying not to show her amazement.

"Is that all?" he replied sounding relieved.

"Pay her at once!" insisted the lady, then added with a whisper, "We can always claim it back."

The man hurriedly dropped two bronze tannas into Molly's hand.

"Thank you!" she said.

"Please can we go now?" asked the lady.

"Er ... yes, of course!" Molly said, rather surprised.

"I wasn't asking you." The lady pointed a heavily gold-ringed finger over Molly's head. "I was asking her."

But by the time Molly looked round, all there was to see behind her was the huge old Sacrifice Tree. Molly shrugged her shoulders and turned back, but the man had already whipped the horses on, and the carriage was hurtling away past the drooling restaurant door and off into the distance.

Molly packed her things away and tried to work out why one moment the couple had been so rude and the next they had been so desperate to buy the bracelet. But in the end she gave up because, after all, why should she care? She had her two bronze tannas and so yippee – it was time to get home.

Grizelda stayed hidden behind the Sacrifice Tree until Molly was safely out of the way, then, slinging her bow back over her shoulder, she went to retrieve her horse from the thicket where she'd left it. As she leapt up on to its back, a broad smile came to her face. Even after all these years as a savage, she still found it amazing how people can change their attitude when they see there's an arrow aimed straight at their neck.

The collector calls

A few days later, Molly was hiding something in the hole under her pink rug and this time it wasn't coins. The hawker had called and when he'd opened his coat of a thousand pockets, she'd seen exactly what she wanted for Urgum, so she had handed over all of her five tannas and got it. Now the present was safely tucked away she found herself breathing a sigh of relief. She had been worried that a tax collector would call while she still had some money, but now that she'd spent it, how could they take it off her?

GOYY-ANGGGG!

The sound from Olk's great gong rang around the cave.

"Go and see who it is, can you Molly?" shouted Urgum from his bedroom. "I'm busy sharpening some axes and doing some other tough stuff."

Actually he wasn't sharpening axes, but the other stuff he was doing was tough – or at least it was for Urgum. Ages ago Molly had shown him what a letter "U" for "Urgum" looked like, but being a true savage he had naturally made a rude noise and shown no interest at all. However, today, Divina and the boys were out foraging for firewood so Urgum had taken the chance to hide away with a copy of *Modern Savage,* and now he was anxiously turning the skin pages and staring at the shapes and symbols to see if he could recognize any "U"s.

Molly had stepped past Olk and out of the mouthway to the cragg, where she was talking to a small grey man on a small grey horse. He was wearing the palace colours and carrying a dull-looking book similar to the one that the dizzalid had been holding. Molly explained that her dad was busy and her mum was out but, to her surprise, the small man did not want either of them.

"Molly of Golgarth?" he said, looking at his dull book.

"That's me," said Molly.

"Manufacturer and purveyor of flower jewellery?"

"Er ... I suppose that's me too." Molly nodded. "So who are you?"

"My name is Mr Perkins from the Department of Tax Collection," said the little man. "And our records show that you have made a further income of two bronze tannas."

"How do you know that?" Molly gasped.

"Somebody submitted a TC 421 to the reclaims department," explained the collector.

"A what?" asked Molly, completely by accident. Even before he opened his mouth she already knew that she was going to be bored silly by the answer.

The collector raised an eyebrow in disbelief. He knew he was only dealing with a little savage child, but surely savages weren't so out of touch with civilization that she didn't know about TC 421 tax reclaim forms! He took a deep breath and started to explain very very slowly.

"Every time somebody buys something, they can submit a TC 421," he said. "This is a form that enables them to reclaim the tax on the value of the purchase..."

Gosh this was boring. Molly's head was starting to spin, her eyes were closing and she almost fell over while the voice droned on and on...

"...and the amount reclaimed is offset by making the transaction cost subject to tax due from the receiver..."

SKUBLUPPAH-BALONK!

High up on the cragg wall, the droning voice reached the two vultures, Djinta and Percy. It sounded so dull that they both immediately dozed off and fell out of their ragged nest.

"...the receiver's tax being classed as income, and therefore applicable at a rate of one half of monies received..."

CLUNG!

Molly opened her eyes and saw that Olk's blade had slumped to the ground and his head had fallen on to his chest. Low, stomach-wobbling snores gently echoed out and floated away across the plains of the Lost Desert. Even the giant sentry had been unable to take any more.

"...and as payment in this instance was two bronze tannas, you owe half of that. So you have to pay me one bronze tanna. It's all quite simple."

At last, the collector's monotonous monologue came to a stop.

Molly blinked and shook her head to wake herself up properly. "Simple as pips," she said. She couldn't wait to tell him what she'd got to say. "There's just one teeny little problem."

"If you've got a problem, I'll go through it all again for you."

"NO!" cried Molly. "No, no, not again! The problem is that I haven't got one bronze tanna."

"How do you mean you haven't got it?" The tax collector slammed his book shut and straightened his back. His eyes had taken on a mean and evil look. "I don't believe you. How can you not have one bronze tanna?"

"I just haven't," said Molly.

"Oh really?" demanded the collector. "I think you're just refusing to pay."

"You can think what you like," said Molly. "All I know is that I haven't got it, so there's nothing we can do about it."

"Oh yes there is!" the collector sneered. He peered through the cragg entrance and over towards their cave. "In cases of non-payment I am empowered to seize goods to the value of the debt, which in your case will be probably be everything you have."

"Oh, keep your vest on," said Molly. "I'll get a tanna some time, so why don't you come back in a few days?"

"Because I'm here NOW!" said the little man, getting excited. "I am Mr Perkins from the Palace and when I come to collect I *never* leave without payment. I'm coming in."

"Hah!" Molly laughed. "Nobody ever gets past Olk!"

But the collector simply nudged his horse forward and rode past the sleeping sentry and into the rock basin. All Molly could do was run after him. Just as Mr Perkins reached the entrance to their cave, Urgum dashed out, clutching the copy of *Modern Savage* magazine.

"Who are you?" they both said to each other in surprise.

"I am Mr Perkins from Tax Collection," said the collector, getting off his horse.

"Oooh, how posh!" said Urgum, not really listening.

The collector stepped into the cave and started taking everything off the shelves and putting them into a large bag, but for some reason Urgum didn't seem to notice. All he could do was walk round after the little man pointing at a copy of *Modern Savage* magazine making loud "ahem" noises. Eventually he got so desperate that he said, "So Mr Posh Perkins, be honest, when were you last featured in *Modern Savage* magazine?"

Molly was standing in the cave entrance and was shocked at what she saw.

"Dad!" she shouted. "What's going on?"

"I'm in *Modern Savage*!" said Urgum, proudly hurrying over to show her the magazine. "Look at this big word. It starts with a big 'U' for 'Urgum'. Well that is a 'U' isn't it?"

Urgum was pointing at a page, and sure enough the big word at the top did start with a "U" for "Urgum". Molly nodded, but before she'd had time to say anything else, Urgum had rushed back to show the page to the collector.

"There!" said Urgum. "Look! That's surprised you, hasn't it Mr tax Perkins posh collector person thing? It's a whole page about ME!"

And indeed, when Mr Perkins looked at the page he was so surprised, he didn't know what to say. "Is that really about you?" he said at last.

"Of course." Urgum carefully folded the magazine and put it on one of the shelves. But then Mr Perkins simply picked it up and put it in his bag.

"Oi!" said Urgum, suddenly realizing that not all was

as it should have been. "What's going on?"

"He wants me to give him one bronze tanna," said Molly. "But I can't so he's come to take away everything we have."

"Oh has he?" said Urgum. "Has he really?"

Urgum snatched the bag from the collector, pulled out the magazine and carefully placed it back on the shelf. Looking into the bag, he gasped. "These are all Divina's bits and pieces!"

"Not any more," said the collector smugly. "I've impounded them because the girl can't pay her tax, and there's not a thing you can do about it."

Urgum looked at the little grey man in front of him and wasn't sure he'd heard him right. But when the little man reached out and tried to take his bag back, Urgum realized that he was quite serious. So Urgum got even seriouser.

"Joke over," he said softly. "Molly, stand well back from the doorway."

"You can't ignore tax, savage," said the collector. "This is official business. I'm only doing my duty."

"Then that's the difference between you and me," said Urgum. "Because what I'm about to do is completely unofficial business, and I'm doing it for fun."

SHTUNK!

Urgum smashed the collector right in the jaw with his fist and sent him flying out of the doorway and halfway across to the mouthway of the basin where he slumped to the ground in a daze.

"That's all you're going to collect from here," called Urgum. "We've had enough of this money number tax thing. See yourself out."

Thinking that would be the end of the matter, Urgum sat down with Molly to show her the "U" in *Modern Savage* magazine again when, to his surprise, he was called for.

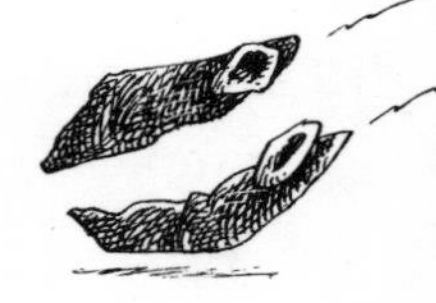

"Oi, savage!" yelled the collector from outside. He was lying on the ground trying to raise himself on to one elbow. "Remember my face because next time you see it, you're a dead man."

Urgum paused. Was it worth sticking his head out of the cave and honouring the little runt with a reply or not? Probably not. He went back to the magazine.

"Did you hear me?" yelled Mr Perkins, obviously thinking that Urgum had too much respect for palace officials to do anything. "You'll die for what you just did."

Urgum sighed and put the magazine back on the shelf.

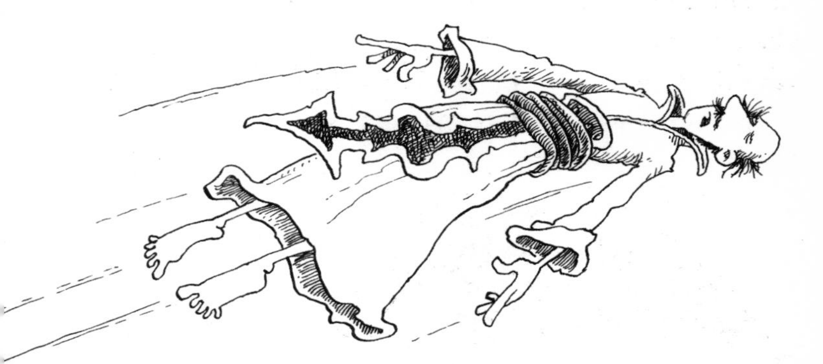

It was no good. You simply didn't go shouting things like that to the fiercest barbarian that the Lost Desert had ever known. Urgum couldn't ignore the man, if only for the sake of his reputation.

"It's no good Molly," he said. "We need a quiet word with this gentleman."

Urgum got to his feet and stepped out of the cave. As the barbarian's heavy shadow loomed across the helpless figure, for the first time in his life, Mr Perkins began to really regret opening his mouth.

"Let me see if I've understood this," said Urgum, scratching his head. "You're still lying where I put you with one small punch. You're all on your own in an enemy compound, you're unarmed, you're a long way from home and yet ... and yet you're still threatening to kill me. What will it take to teach you some respect? Is there any reason why I don't just twist your head around a few times until it comes off?"

"Of course there's a reason!" said Mr Perkins. "I have the full authority of the State on my side. You can't touch me."

"Authority of the State!" Urgum laughed. He waved his hand around to indicate the rocky basin. It was strewn with bones, a couple of ostriches were arguing over a dead snake and Mungoid's emergency pants were hanging on the Lynching Tree. There wasn't much sign of State, let alone any authority.

Urgum laughed again. "You're a very funny bloke, do you know that?"

"Don't laugh at me!" Mr Perkins scowled. "I WILL kill you!"

That's when Urgum stopped laughing. The collector suddenly saw a huge hand reaching down towards him so he frantically tried to scrabble away but he was too late. Urgum grabbed his shoulder and hauled him up so that the collector's face was within snapping distance of the savage's sharpened teeth.

Mr Perkins braced himself to be utterly gnashed, mashed and bashed until he realized that the savage was dusting the dirt down off his clothes, and had even smoothed his hair back for him.

"I underestimated you." Urgum stepped back, eyeing him with respect. "You're a very brave little fellow."

Molly came out, picked up his squashed hat and pushed it back into shape. When it was ready she handed it to Urgum who placed it on his head, and then carefully set it straight.

"Lovely," declared Urgum. "What a smart little softhand you are."

"You don't seem to take me seriously!" the collector whimpered.

"Oh I do." Urgum nodded. "I take all of you seriously."

"All of who?" asked the collector, as Urgum hoisted him up on to his horse.

"All the people who say they want to kill me," explained Urgum. "There's an awful lot of them and, trust me, every one of them is a lot bigger and nastier than you. What's more, some of them have been waiting to kill me for a very long time so if you kill me first, you'll be upsetting a lot of very strange and unpleasant people."

"But it's my right to kill you!" said the collector, snivelling.

"It won't make much difference to them," said Urgum. "In fact if you do kill me, I wouldn't want to be you when the others come looking for you."

He slapped the backside of the horse and sent it cantering off towards the mouthway of the cragg with the collector still muttering his pitiful little threats.

"I bet that's the last we see of him, Dad!" Molly laughed. "That was so brilliant sending him off with that lie about all those others wanting to kill you."

"Lie?" asked Urgum, confused. "What lie was that then?"

On the shelf inside the cave, the magazine was lying next to two strange little god statues. Unseen by anyone, their eyes flickered into life. Tangor and Tangal exchanged worried glances.

"Our joke was all going so well!" moaned Tangal. "Molly's really quietened him down. He hasn't picked any stupid fights or taken any ridiculous risks..."

"...if only she hadn't tried to teach him how to read!" agreed Tangor. "It's bad enough that he should be looking for the letter 'U' in *Modern Savage* magazine, but why did he have to find this...?"

The gods shuddered as they recalled how the tax collector had said "Is that really about you?" and their proud barbarian champion had proudly said "Yes".

"We must do something before Urgum shows this to anybody else," said Tangor.

"We could just tear the page out," said Tangal.

"Never!" said Tangor. "If Urgum found it missing he'd go berserk. Thousands could die in mindless carnage. We'll have to change it."

"But that'll involve moving all the ink on the page around, atom by atom!" said Tangal.

"We've no choice." Tangor sighed. "If anyone tells him what this really says he'll die of embarrassment, and then he'll be up to join us at our table and you know what that means."

And so the gods started the long painful task of moving trillions and trillions of ink atoms around the page, but at least it was easier than feeding Urgum for ever.

A Secret Sale

The following day, Molly set off back to her place by the crossroads with her flower jewellery. Ahead of her the entire desert plain looked utterly devoid of likely customers; it was too hot, and Molly was already fed up. As she walked up the last bit of Smiley Alley, she noticed that in the distance the Giant Juppotan plant was also looking fed up and neglected. Its entire body had wilted over and the sound membranes had flopped down and were hanging off its back, listlessly swaying in the breeze. But the plant must have been aware of her approach because by the time she had seated herself, the restaurant door was open, the membranes had tightened up enough to make noises, and the smells were drifting towards her.

There was not a soul about, so Molly lay back on the warm sand, having first checked it for burrowed snakes. High above, she saw the pet vultures Djinta and Percy circling.

Better not go to sleep! she thought with a grin, knowing how they liked to swoop on anything they thought might be dead. But staying awake was difficult. The music from the restaurant door sounded like a slow ballad which didn't seem to start or end, it just crooned comfortably along and very soon Molly's eyelids began to close. "Tum-tee tumty doo dah..." she hummed along and then she was asleep.

As the sun slowly moved across the sky, the music played on and the vultures gradually circled lower and lower. But, unknown to either the vultures or Molly, the real danger was creeping across the ground.

"Molly?" called a distant voice. "Molly, where are you?"

Molly woke with a jolt. How long had she drifted off for? And what was that tickling sensation around her ankle? As she reached to scratch it, she looked down.

A long sticky grey tendril had sprouted from the doorway of the Juppotan and reached its way right across the sand towards her. The very end of the tendril had a tiny pink tip covered in fine sensory hairs which were brushing against her skin, picking up her scent. The sound from the doorway was getting wilder and the whole thing was beginning to quiver in excitement.

Even as she looked at it, the tendril was getting thicker and stronger and was starting to ooze with sticky saliva. She watched with awed fascination as slowly and silently the end rose up in the air and got ready to snap itself around her leg and drag her away into the digestive cavities of the plant. It was so interesting that Molly quite forgot how hard Grizelda had found it to detach herself from that vile green slime. In fact, she only remembered just as the tendril was reaching back, preparing to strike. Quickly, she grabbed a sharp rock and splattered the delicate pink tip to a pulp. The tendril shot back, the giant doorway mouth slammed shut and the membranes made a noise that sounded suspiciously like "Oh knickers".

"Sorry, plant," muttered Molly under her breath. "I keep messing up your plans. But maybe I'll make it up to you one day."

She heard the distant voice again. "Molly!"

"Here!" she called back.

A large figure came ambling down the path from the direction of the cragg towards her. It was Robbin, the largest brother, and he had brought with him a flask of water and some sweet scrunchy burnt bits of something from the kitchen floor. (It was hard to tell what some of the scrunchy burnt bits from the kitchen floor had been before they got burnt, but who cared? Once they were burnt and scrunchy, they were utterly yummy, so that's all that mattered.)

"How's it going, little sis?" he asked, slowly lowering himself to sit beside her and offering her a drink and a bit of scrunch.

"Not too well," said Molly. "Nobody's passing. I still need just one bronze tanna to pay the tax, or they'll come in and seize everything we've got."

"So what are you selling?"

"Flower brooches and necklaces," said Molly. "Or I can put them on pins and make earrings."

Robbin took a small piece of scrunch between his fat thumb and forefinger and nibbled it neatly as he looked over Molly's display. *Robbin is always very neat,* thought Molly. Of course it would be foolish to forget that he was also a tough barbaric merciless blood-thirsty savage, but if you could do all that and still manage to be neat, then that was pretty cool. Molly decided that when she had grown up to be the fiercest barbarian ever, she would make sure she was the neatest barbarian ever too, which would then mean she was the coolest barbarian ever. Even Grizelda would be impressed at that!

"How did you do that one?" Robbin pointed at a smart little red pansy trapped inside a clear, yellowy stone.

"I used a bit of amber from the Sacrifice Tree," explained Molly. "It's like honey that seeps out of the wood. I just wiped a bit on the flower and left it in the sun, and it went hard enough to make a nice badge. It came out well, didn't it?"

"How much is it?" asked Robbin.

"One bronze tanna," said Molly. "Everything is. I just need one bronze tanna."

"I'll take it then," said Robbin and he held out his hand. In it was a bronze tanna.

Molly gasped. "Where did you get that from?"

"I found it when I was a baby," said Robbin. "And ever since then I've been secretly saving it."

"You don't have to give it to me, Robbin," exclaimed Molly. "If you want the badge, you can just have it. Save your money for something you really like."

"That's what I really like," said Robbin simply. "Besides, as Dad said, stupid flowers are what all the hard boys are wearing these days."

Gently he took Molly's hand in his own great fingers and slipped her the little coin. Then carefully he picked up the small red flower badge and pinned it inside his shirt.

"I ... I don't know what to say," said Molly.

"Probably better if you don't say anything," said Robbin, indicating the cave. "You know what the others are like."

And, yes, Molly did know what her other brothers were like, so she promised Robbin that nobody would ever know who gave her that last bronze tanna or what it was for.

The Defenders of Golgarth

A few days later, as luck would have it, the cragg's fresh meat supplies ran out, so Urgum, Mungoid and Grizelda went off to track down the Wandering Jungle. This was a massive lush area which had a mean habit of moving around, but it was well worth the effort to find it because it was full of large, exotic and ridiculously delicious creatures.

Back in the basin everybody else was getting on with the usual boring chores that need to be done

in every good home. Ruff and Ruinn's chore involved climbing up the ladders to the high ledge over the mouthway to the cragg. A row of massive boulders had been carefully balanced along this ledge and each boulder had a few iron bands wrapped around it with a nasty selection of long dirty spikes sticking out.

Ruff had the chore of sharpening the spikes with a file while Ruinn checked the boulders were still loose enough to push off the edge. Far below them was the area of ground directly in front of where Olk stood. Of course, nothing could ever get past Olk (apart from extremely boring tax collectors) but just in case, there was always the enjoyable **WEEEE-SPLADGE** option.

Once the boulders had been all checked and primed, Ruff and Ruinn came down and headed back to the cave where Robbin was helping Divina and Molly in the kitchen, preparing a batch of sauce to go with whatever dead thing was going to arrive for tea. Raymond's bags were by the fire and from one of them his hand was sticking out, holding a toasting fork with a large mushroom on the end.

What made it particularly peaceful was the fact that Rekk and Rakk were up in the watchtower so nobody could hear them fighting. (There was also another son in the cave somewhere but nobody knew what he was doing or cared much.)

Everything was relaxed and quiet and so Ruff offered to sing everyone a ballad he'd made up about how brave and daring he was, and so Ruinn offered to rip out his tongue and stick it on the end of Raymond's toasting fork and so Ruff decided not to sing after all and everything remained relaxed and quiet. But it wasn't going to stay that way for long.

In the corner of the cave was a brass tube that came out of the floor, on the end of which was fitted a small trumpet. The tube ran under the sand, out of the cave, right around the basin, over the rocks and all the way up to the top of the watchtower, where a similar trumpet was fixed to the other end. Up on the watchtower platform the twins Rekk and Rakk had been passing the time by having a strangling competition, when they spotted a party of horsemen coming down from the far end of Smiley Alley.

"Look, soldiers!" Rakk gasped as Rekk's hand closed over his windpipe.

"Wow – and coming this way!" Rekk belched, with Rakk's hand still tight around his neck.

"I'll tell the others." Rekk let go of Rakk and reached for the trumpet tube.

"No way!" Rakk squeezed his brother's throat even harder.

But Rekk managed to grab the tube and blow into it, sending a signal down to the cave.

PFARRRTUMMMP!

The brass trumpet in the cave sounded, making everybody jump.

Ruinn ran across and spoke down it. "What's happening?"

From the end of the trumpet the twins' voices echoed around the cave.

"There's someone coming!" **KRUNCH** "Gerroff, I'm telling. There's ten guards from the palace." **SLAPPP** "Nah! It's more like fifty and they're all armed." **BIFF** "It's not fifty, it's more like two million..." **WALLOP STOMP**.

"Thanks," said Ruinn. "I think we understood that."

The noise brought Robbin through from the kitchen and, as he listened, he stirred some sauce in a small pan. "Dad'll be cross he's not here if there's soldiers coming!" he said.

"I don't think we need your father," said Divina. "Do we?"

"NO!"

"Right boys," said Divina. "I need you up on the ledge in case we need to drop the spiked boulders on them..."

The boys all dashed to the cave entrance.

"...but I need one volunteer to stay here and stir the sauce. I'm not having it ruined just because of an armed attack."

Robbin hurriedly thrust his spoon at Ruinn who thrust it at Ruff who thrust it at the other son who snatched Raymond's toasting fork away and replaced it with the spoon.

"Raymond volunteers!" The boys cheered, then charged out of the cave, across the basin and up the rope ladders that hung from the top of the cragg wall.

"Aw!" said Raymond's voice from one of his other bags. "It's always me."

"Never mind, Raymond," said Molly. "I'll put a sword

in your other hand so you can still feel you're part of the fun."

"Oh yippee." Raymond moaned. "Me and a pot of sauce. What a grand fight that'll be."

Molly was keen to get out to join Olk and see what was going on, but Divina had hurried off down the corridor.

"Come on, Mother," shouted Molly. "What's keeping you?"

"Found it!" cried Divina triumphantly from within her bedroom. "Just coming!"

"What's she found?" Raymond asked Molly.

"I dunno," admitted Molly. "Maybe she's had a really nasty poison-tipped dagger hidden away somewhere."

"Or a long spiked whip," said Raymond.

At that moment Divina dashed back, one hand pushing a final silver comb into her immaculate hair and the other clutching a small red stick.

"What's that?" said Molly.

"My best lipstick," said Divina quickly puckering up and slapping a bit on. "After all, it isn't every day we get attacked by people from the palace. Although we might have to crush, massacre and destroy them, we don't want them going away thinking that we're completely uncivilized."

The Man from Accounts Pending

Divina and Molly stood beside Olk in the mouthway to the cragg, and on the ledge high above them, the boys had taken up their positions by the spiked boulders. Everyone was pulling their meanest faces except Divina who was smiling sweetly and being the perfect hostess. Outside, across the plain, and keeping well back from Olk, was a mixed bunch of about twenty armed riders wearing palace guard uniforms, none of which seemed to quite fit properly.

"I said I'd be back," said a voice from the group. "And I am."

"And who are you exactly?" called Divina.

"I'm sure the girl remembers me," said the little grey man on his little grey horse as he pushed his way through to the front. "I am Mr Perkins from Tax Collection and these people with me are the Tax Territorials."

"The WHO?" everybody said as they looked at the strange bunch, nearly all of whom were wearing a hat three sizes too big.

"The Tax Territorials," said Mr Perkins. "They are all volunteers from the office who have been on an extensive evening course in fighting. What you see before you is a fully-qualified squadron of hardened troops. I warn you, every single one of them has passed their toughness exams, and some of them even got merits and distinctions."

"GRRRR!" said all the Tax Territorials to show how tough they were.

"Oooh – scary!" The boys sniggered on the ledge above them.

"You may laugh," said Mr Perkins, "but we've come to collect the bronze tanna that's owing, or you're all under arrest and your goods will be seized."

"Keep your pants dry," said Molly. "I've got it!"

Molly walked out past Olk to where the collector was sitting on his horse, then pulled the bronze tanna from her pocket and flicked it up at him. Mr Perkins caught it in his hand and looked extremely disappointed.

"There, tax paid," she said. "So goodbye then."

"Not so fast young madam," he shouted. "I've a score to settle with your father. He assaulted me, a tax official of the palace."

"He's out," said Molly, who had picked a clump of grass growing in a niche in the rocks and was offering it to the little grey horse.

"Is he really?" snapped Mr Perkins. "I've come to kill him. I said I would and now I'm here to do it."

"Oh what a shame," said Divina who was still standing in the mouthway of the cragg and smiling sweetly. "He'll be so sorry he missed you. Perhaps you'd like to pop back and kill him another time?"

"I do NOT pop back." The tax collector snarled. "How long will he be out for exactly?"

"I've no idea." Divina sighed apologetically. "But if you need to tottle off, I'll tell him you called."

"Yeah, tottle off!" shouted the boys from the ledge. "Go on! Bye-bye!"

"We'll wait as long as it takes," yelled Mr Perkins.

But the other territorials were already turning their horses away from the cragg. One of them (Mr Wiggins from Accounting Personnel Management) called over:

"We really ought to make a move, sir. There's that important financial strategy seminar tomorrow morning," he said, and then added proudly, "I'm in charge of putting out the pencils and paper."

Mr Perkins gave him such a filthy look that Mr Wiggins thought it best to do a smart salute. Unfortunately his sleeve was far longer than his arm and he just ended up slapping himself in the eye with the cuff which made the boys laugh so much...

"Ho ho ho..."

...that they nearly fell off the ledge.

"...EEEK!"

Mr Perkins hissed in disappointment but then he glanced at the bronze tanna in his hand and an evil smile spread across his face.

"HOLD IT!" he shouted at his squadron, who stopped and turned back, even though they didn't know what they were supposed to be holding. "There's one more little matter to clear up first."

The tax collector leant over to Molly who was gently stroking his horse's nose.

"Where did this tanna come from?" he asked suspiciously.

"I sold a flower badge," said Molly.

"So you earnt it!" said Mr Perkins triumphantly.

"Well whoopee-doo for you," said Molly. "Of course I earnt it."

"If you earnt it, you owe tax on it." Mr Perkins grinned, rubbing his hands. The other riders had now returned and gathered around excitedly.

"How can I owe tax on it when I've just given it to you?" asked Molly.

"This tanna pays for the tax you already owed," said Mr Perkins. "But you haven't paid any tax on the tanna itself so you owe another half tanna. Arrest her."

A couple of women in giant green trousers clambered down from their horses. With great excitement, Mrs Pottersnitch and Miss Tibbly from the Receipt Docketing Department grabbed some heavy chains and hurried over to Molly, but Molly had no intention of being chained up if she could help it.

"Hang on!" she said to them. "There might be tax to pay on that tanna, but it's not my tanna any more." She pointed at Mr Perkins who was smugly tossing the little coin up in the air. "He's the one that's got it now, but he

hasn't paid the tax on it so he's the one you should be arresting."

The territorials glanced at each other then towards Mr Perkins in confusion. The delay was all Molly needed to slip away from the group.

"Don't let that little girl make fools of you!" snapped the tax collector. "Grab her!"

But Molly had already ducked behind Olk and as the squadron moved towards him the great blade twitched.

"I'm so sorry," said Divina in her perfect-hostess voice. "But if you come any closer, one sweep of our sentry's blade will remove your heads."

"And that's not all," said Molly. "Take a look up there."

On the ledge high above the mouthway to the cragg, the boys had started to push on the spiked boulders and had got them rocking and creaking ominously. A few little stones had already come loose and were plummeting down, bouncing off the cragg wall and into the faces of the territorials, who backed away nervously. Their evening course obviously hadn't dealt with how to survive being crushed by an avalanche of spiked boulders.

Mr Perkins was furious, and it didn't help that Divina was still smiling sweetly at him with her head coyly tilted to one side.

"Madam," he said, trying to sound reasonable. "I can see that you understand how things are done in the civilized world."

"Why, thank you!" exclaimed Divina, delighted.

"Obviously, this position needs explaining a little more clearly," continued the tax collector, "and therefore I think it would help if I introduced you to one of my colleagues."

"Oh, I should be honoured!"

Divina quickly reached to her hair and checked that

her silver combs were in place. A gap appeared in the ranks of the territorials as they made way for someone or something to come through from behind. Slowly a small but very powerful tugpony came into view. Its six short legs were like tree trunks and although tugponies were not fast, they were in great demand at circuses where people cheered to see them dragging elephants backwards.

But however odd the tugpony looked, the rider was even odder.

"Great Gollarks!" muttered Ruff, up above. "What's that?"

"This..." said the collector with a huge smug grin on his face, "...this is Mr Thompkinson from Accounts Pending. And as your account *is* pending, Mr Thompkinson will deal with you."

Mr Thompkinson's appearance could be summed up in one word: solid. Just like the tugpony that carried him, he was wider than he was tall and the muscles in his limbs bulged like melons. His green uniform was so stretched that it was barely recognizable, and his head was so flat that it looked like his neck just had a patterned lid on it.

"Mr Thompkinson will make the position clear once

he's been properly introduced," said Mr Perkins. "So say how do you do."

Mr Thomkinson rode up towards the mouthway to the cragg and held out his thick muscular hand. Instinctively, Divina stepped forward past Olk and shook it.

"How do you do, Mr Thompkinson," she said.

The mouth on the top of the fat neck grinned.

"There!" The tax collector smiled. "And now the position is clear. Mr Thompkinson doesn't let go until your outstanding tax is paid or, ahem ... other arrangements are made."

Divina tried to pull her hand away, but it was hopeless. Mr Thompkinson's grip was like iron. She felt such a fool holding hands with this odd little man who even on the back of his tughorse was barely higher than she was.

"And what precisely happens now?" she demanded.

"We're coming in," said Mr Perkins simply. "We seize your property and if you resist, we arrest you all and sell you into slavery."

Mr Perkins ordered his squadron to approach, although he kept well back himself. From the ledge high above, the boys watched the group nervously edging forwards and wondered what to do. They daren't drop the boulders while their mother was directly underneath and the collector knew it.

He looked up and smiled. "Don't do anything silly, boys!" He sniggered.

"Can't Olk stop them?" whispered Ruff.

"How?" replied Robbin. "That little bloke is holding Mum right in front of him. If Olk sweeps his sword across, he's as likely to hit her as anything."

Eventually, all the territorials assembled behind Mr Thompkinson on the tugpony.

"Password!" boomed Olk.

"Let them past, fatty," said the collector, "or I'll have you down the sulphur mines."

In the mouthway of the cragg Olk shuddered. He hated being called fat. Admittedly he *used* to be fat but since then he'd got a lot bigger and was proud of it. How he would have liked to sweep his great blade around – but Divina was still being held firmly by Mr Thompkinson. If only he knew what to do. Then Olk suddenly became aware of a strange itching. Molly had leapt up and grabbed the back of his belt then pulled herself up and was now scrambling up on to his shoulder. She put her head deep inside his ear and whispered something. Olk's muscles suddenly bulged and creaked. The mighty blade swung upwards from his shoulder until it was pointing directly at the overhead sun. Molly jumped down from his shoulder and stepped back. High above, the boys were peering down off the ledge.

Ruff gasped. "He's put his sword up!"

"I've never seen him do that before," said Ruinn. "He must be letting them in!"

"Oh no!" said Robbin. "What will happen to my sauce?"

"Relax," said Ruinn. "Raymond's guarding it."

"Phew!" Robbin sighed. "I was worried for a moment."

Down below the collector was getting more impatient.

"Go on troops!" he commanded. "The big lump knows when he's beaten. He's letting you through."

But, at that moment, Molly pulled a bag from behind her back which she had already been to fetch from the cave.

"Now Raymond!" she whispered to the bag.

A hand came out of the bag, clutching a glowing red-hot spoon. With a deft flick of the wrist, a white blob of boiling sauce flew at Mr Thomkinson and hit him *SPLOP* squarely in the eye.

"YEEE-OWK!" said Mr Thompkinson of Accounts Pending.

For just a moment he released his grip on Divina, but the tugpony standing directly in front of Olk was the first to realize what was happening next...

SCABBALOTCH!

The tugpony managed to duck its head just in time as the great blade came swinging downwards. It sliced right through the top of Mr Thompkinson's flat head from front to back and passed straight down, neatly dividing his nose in two. Without the slightest hesitation, Olk's sword continued on through the entire body, smoothly splitting it into two symmetrical parts and the blade only came to a stop when it was a hair's width above the tugpony's saddle.

The two halves of Mr Thompkinson from Accounts Pending then slithered down either side of the unharmed tugpony and crumpled on to the ground.

Olk raised the blade once more and brought it back to rest against his shoulder as casually as if he had just swatted a fly.

The tugpony calmly toddled past Olk into the safety of the basin. He knew whose side he wanted to be on if it came to a fight. As Divina quickly followed him in, the first of the spiked boulders landed on Mrs Pottersnitch and Miss Tibbly from the Receipt Docketing Department neatly squashing them into the ground. The other boulders followed and the rest of the squadron galloped backwards as fast as they could from the cragg, just leaving the horrified tax collector trying to control all the words that had jumped into his mouth at once.

"You, just you ... you wait ... just wait, just ... you just, just...!" screamed Mr Perkins. "You wait, you just wait. You just wait until you see what I'm going to do now!"

"What are you going to do?" shouted Molly.

"I'm going to fill in an F28," said Mr Perkins.

The territorials gasped. "Not an F28!"

"What's an F28?" called Ruinn from up on the ledge.

"Don't any of you idiots know what an F28 is?" the tax collector sneered, not expecting an answer. High on the ledge, the boys looked at each other blankly because they didn't expect an answer either.

"Yes, I know. It's an official form," said a mystery

voice that seemed to come from right beside them.

"Eh?" said the boys nervously. It took a moment for them to realize where the voice had come from. It was the seventh son: the Other One – he had actually spoken! This was really creepy because they hadn't even noticed he was on the ledge with them and, what was worse, he had probably been there all the time. Would he speak again? What would he say? It was all too unnerving but thankfully that was as far as he got.

"Oi, I'll tell them if you don't mind, thank you *so* much!" shouted the tax collector, annoyed that the

seventh son was about to steal his big important announcement. He cleared his throat and put on his grandest voice. "An F28 authorizes me to deploy the entire Tax Territorial Army. From now on, no more civilized introductions or friendly visits. From now on, this is WAR!"

The tax collector was looking very pleased with himself until he noticed that Divina was beside Olk, smiling sweetly again.

"How lovely," she called out as she waved him off. "In the meantime, mind how you go!"

The Mystery of the Spiked Boulders

As the rest of the day wore on, there was still no sign of Urgum, Mungoid and Grizelda, so the sun gave up waiting and started to set behind a distant volcano at the edge of the Forgotten Crater. Orange beams of light shone through the sulphur fumes, shimmered right across the cooling sands and finally hit the cragg wall, creating giant ghostly figures that writhed and twisted all the way from the ground up to the high ledge along the top. But what was even more disturbing than the ghostly figures was the boys' method of replacing the spiked boulders they had dropped on the Tax Territorials that afternoon.

They all stood along the high ledge, clutching one end of a rope which passed through a large pulley fixed over their heads. The other end of the rope reached down to the ground where it was tied around a boulder. Ruff would shout "One two three ... jump!" and together they would all leap off, still clutching the rope. As they went down, the boulder would be pulled up, bouncing off the wall as it rose (and usually giving them all a good bashing as it passed them) and then finally it would come to rest on the ledge.

At least that's what was supposed to happen, but by the time they had got to the last boulder, everybody else had got so bored of Ruff giving the orders that when he shouted "One two three ... jump!" for the final time, they all secretly let go. Ruff jumped off by himself and as he wasn't heavy enough on his own to raise the boulder, he just ended up dangling from the end of rope in mid-air. Ha ha ha.

"What am I supposed to do now?" said Ruff crossly, but the others had all climbed down and gone off to finish their laughing somewhere else. The only one left was Raymond whose bags were still on the ledge just above where Ruff was hanging.

"Want me to get you down?" asked Raymond's voice

from one of the bags.

"And what can you do, chopped-up boy?" said Ruff meanly.

"If you're going to be rude," said Raymond, "you can work out how to get down yourself, but I wouldn't advise letting go. It's a long drop and you'd make a big splatt at the bottom."

Ruff swung and kicked and cursed, and finally gave in.

"Well?" he demanded, then added, "Please?"

It was simple when Raymond explained.

"All you do is swing across to where the other end of the rope that's connected to the boulder is hanging down from the pulley. Grab that bit of rope *but don't let go of the rope you were holding or it will fly up through the pulley and you'll fall.* Instead, knot the end of the first rope to the other bit. THEN you can slide down safely."

Ruff worked out what to do next for himself. You go and find all your other brothers who are sitting on the rocks in the basin still laughing at you and you tell them that you escaped without any help. Then, after a very long time, you manage to convince them to come with you and get the last boulder up on the ledge. And then when you get there you feel really stupid because the last

boulder is already up on the ledge because somehow Raymond has managed it himself. And then everybody thinks Raymond has magic powers and you are a complete idiot and they start laughing at you again.

Of course Raymond didn't have magic powers (although he didn't tell them that), he was just like any other perfectly normal dismembered person living in a selection of bags. The truth is that Raymond's mouth had whistled for Mr Thompkinson's tugpony, which had spent the afternoon wandering around peacefully looking for bits of cactus to chew. One of Raymond's arms groped its way over to a second piece of rope lying on the ledge and tied it on to the first piece, doubling the length. Then the arm grabbed on to the new rope, wiggled itself off the ledge, slid down as far as Ruff's knot and undid it. The arm continued to slide to the ground and passed the long loose end of the rope to the friendly tugpony, who took it in his mouth.

The arm scrambled on to the boulder, the mouth whistled, and with minimum effort the tugpony hoisted the boulder up to the ledge. The arm then hopped off the boulder and back into its bag. All very simple really because, as Molly had said on first meeting him, Raymond was the one with a brain.

The Savage and the Softhand III

As the boulders were being reset, Molly was sitting on the four-poster bed in her parents' room, watching Divina snatching things up, shaking them out and putting them down in different places just for the sake of it. The blazing torch on the wall was spitting, sparking and hissing, which was a good impression of Divina's mood. She was obviously still a bit huffy about the hand-shaking incident, and Molly was wondering what to say to make her feel better.

"I tell you something, Mum," said Molly. "You were pretty cool today."

"I didn't feel cool," snapped Divina.

"Of course you were!" said Molly. "You're always cool. After all, Mungoid says you're the only person who ever made Dad wash his face and lived."

"You did it too," said Divina.

"Er, yes..." said Molly uncertainly, "...but Mungoid said that you did it better. Go on, Mum, tell me what happened."

Divina did a sharp sniff but then realized that Molly was trying to be nice, so she relaxed slightly.

"Sorry Molly," she said. "I can't tell you. It was a long time ago, and it was such a nasty event that if anyone were to hear about it, they'd be sick."

"Wow, that must have been really gross!" exclaimed Molly with great joy.

"It was," said Divina. "It was our wedding day, but I can't tell you or you'll be sick."

"Oh Mum!" pleaded Molly. "I've seen Dad take his trousers off in the lounge! If I can take that, then I can take anything. So go on, tell me, PLEASE..."

Divina sighed, then sat herself on the bed beside her daughter. Molly had to know sometime, she supposed, so this might as well be it.

She started by explaining that one of the best parts about marrying Urgum had been the sheer fun of shocking all the tedious, pointless, know-nothing, pompous softhands such as Mr Perkins who lived on committees, were pampered by slave labour, died in their sleep and were buried under statues of themselves paid for with poor people's taxes. At the wedding ceremony itself, in terms of shock value, Urgum had excelled himself. But as Molly was to find out, in terms of shock value, Divina had excelled herself too.

The wedding was held in a massive banqueting marquee which had been set up in the Laplace water gardens. About three hundred "very closest" friends of Divina's family had been invited to the ceremony, but Urgum himself had arrived alone. There had been some talk of letting him bring his oldest and bestest friend, Mungoid the Ungoid, but the matrimonial planning committee headed by Gastan had regretfully decided that one extra guest would make things far too crowded and could pose a public health hazard. Urgum hadn't objected for fear of losing his bride, but Divina had secretly been furious on his behalf. She'd said nothing for fear of delaying the proceedings: all that mattered to her was that the ceremony lasted long enough for Urgum to become her legal husband and then she would be free of the whole smarmy softhand class for life.

The ceremony was conducted by the Matramam, a kindly female official wearing the green and golden robes of the Laplace Palace. She officiated over all manner of weddings and she didn't even blink at the extraordinary sight of the immacuately-coiffured girl being betrothed

to the hulking great sweaty barbarian. But then why would she? As weddings go, it was quite straightforward – only two people were involved and neither of them were dead or were being forced to declare their oaths with a sword tip pressed to their necks.

The service went smoothly and the Matramam was just about to reach that sensitive moment when she would announce to the couple, "You may now exchange a breath." At this point the bride and groom would bring their noses together and then they'd take turns breathing out while the other breathed in. It wasn't the sort of thing that older people would ever do, but for young people in the first buzz of passion it was a very exciting and significant gesture. Sometimes you could catch them sniffing and snorting in each other's faces for hours.

Anyway, the smiling Matramam was just about to say the required words when, as luck would have it, a huge rogue unicorn barged its way into the marquee.

(Actually luck had nothing to do with it. The Barbarian Gods had been a bit dismayed to see their champion complying with this softhand ceremony so meekly, and so they'd arranged a little surprise to liven up the proceedings.)

The unicorn had the most wonderful time, running amok, rearing and crashing down on the loaded feast tables and poisoning the air with its lung-ripping scent. Its horn was as long as a battle pike and the pores along the barbed tip seeped caustic green acidpus, so it was no wonder that all the softhands were running away and screaming. As they cowered in the corners and under tables, they all took it for granted that Urgum, being the only savage in the place, would feel obliged to save them because they were precious softhands and he

wasn't. The fact that he would be alone and unarmed (Divina's parents had snootily forbidden Urgum from bringing his axe to the wedding) and would probably be crushed by the hooves, disembowelled by the horn and liquefied by the acidpus didn't trouble them in the slightest. All that mattered was that the unicorn should somehow be dealt with and that there would be enough of the feast left unspoilt for them to continue the wedding party with or without the bridegroom.

It was only Divina who spared Urgum any thought.

Gently laying her hand on his arm, she told him that he didn't have to prove anything to her, but at that time she hadn't quite grasped what sort of man she was marrying. As Urgum strode out towards the rampaging beast, Divina was horrified, thinking that she was going to make the move from maiden to widow without any wife time in between. She needn't have worried. On seeing Urgum approach, the surprised beast paused and, for a few moments, the barbarian and the unicorn faced up to each other in a brief gesture of mutual respect. Then, just as all the softhands started to mutter in bored voices, "Get on with it, savage, the sausages are getting cold," the unicorn dropped its head and charged. But it was too late – Urgum had already dived head first between its legs and emerged at the back end. A few seconds later the feast was saved but all the softhands had completely lost their appetities. Urgum had driven the beast screaming away into the night by sinking his sharpened teeth into the very top of the unicorn's tail and biting it right off.

"You may now exchange a breath," the Matramam said, once Urgum had rejoined Divina in front of her, but hardly anyone heard. The softhands had either fainted or were throwing up. From a far corner Divina's

cousin Beldath was bleating at Urgum, "You should be ashamed of yourself. I saw what you did to that poor defenceless creature."

But as far as Urgum and Divina were concerned, they were alone in the room. Urgum brought his face to hers. He was looking so pleased with himself, and as much as she was thrilled with him, Divina knew that if she let him spend the first few seconds of his married life looking so smug and triumphant, it would never wear off. She had to do something.

"Well?" he said, his big nose all ready.

"Wash your face first," she said.

"WHAT?????"

"Wash your face."

"Why? What's wrong with it?"

Divina looked at his face carefully. It was craggy, splattered in blood, smeared with unicorn dung, and it still had a few yellowed tail hairs stuck to it but she didn't notice any of that. All she saw were two surprisingly bright green eyes – so powerful, yet so desperate to please her. There was nothing wrong at all with her new husband's face, but she wasn't going to let him know that.

"You wash your face," she said softly, "and then I'm all yours." She gave him a coy smile and a wink and before he even knew it, the freshly scrubbed Urgum was exchanging a breath with his new wife.

"Oh that's really gross!" said Molly, when Divina had finished giving her the finer details of the wedding ceremony. "You said it was nasty but ... oh, I feel like sick."

"I knew I shouldn't have told you about biting off the unicorn's tail," admitted Divina.

"Oh that's all right," said Molly, trying not to choke. "But exchanging a breath? You and Dad? You actually *did* it? Yuk! I mean, no offence but ... breath? You two? You're so ... OLD! Oh, that's total vommo!"

Swords, Spikes and Sausage Rolls

The following afternoon, the cave kitchen was buzzing with excitement. Urgum, Mungoid and Grizelda had hauled a very rare spotted hippo back to Golgarth, and had hacked it into a giant kebab which was now hanging over the great fire.

Everyone gathered in the shadowy room to watch the flames leap up and wrap themselves around the massive lumps of dripping meat. Mungoid was especially excited because Grizelda was sitting on a bench, staring into the fire with the light reflecting off her river of red hair and looking gorgeously bored ... and there was an empty space right beside her! He was standing over by the far wall and had already smoothed down the three hairs that usually stuck out of the top of his head. He was desperately trying to work out if there was enough room on the empty bit of bench for his bottom, but he knew he wasn't brave enough to go across and try it unless the moment was exactly right.

Only Ruinn was missing – it was his turn to be in the watchtower – but the rest of the boys were merrily describing to Urgum what had happened the previous day.

"You should have seen it, Dad!" said Rakk.

"Right down the middle!" said Rekk.

"Split Mr Thompkinson into two matching pieces," said Rakk.

"Olk must win the prize for most gruesome death of the year!" said Rekk.

"Yeah," agreed Rakk. "It was truly gruesome."

For the first time in their lives the twins had agreed on something.

"Gruesome?" Urgum scoffed. "Now don't get carried away. Yes Olk's good, but if you're looking for gruesome death, I'm your man."

"Pah!" Mungoid snorted. "You're all talk, Urgum. I'm sure Grizelda could do a much more gruesome death than you if she wanted to."

Having paid her this huge compliment, Mungoid felt the moment had come to take a cautious step towards that empty bit of bench. He took a deep breath and raised his leg.

"Gruesome death's not my style," said Grizelda. Mungoid's leg immediately froze with his foot in mid-air and he was sure that everybody in the whole world was staring at him and he felt really rotten.

"But I'm sure Mungoid can do really gruesome deaths," said Grizelda looking at him and although she didn't smile, she didn't not smile either. Then to Mungoid's delight she budged along the bench a bit making the empty space definitely big enough for his bottom. Still holding the same deep breath (and still feeling that everybody in the whole world was staring at him) Mungoid managed to walk over and ease himself down beside Grizelda who didn't get up and move away even though his elbow nearly touched hers. *Wow!*

Meanwhile, across the kitchen, Divina was thumbing wistfully through a copy of *Modern Savage*. She was checking on the most suitable wine to drink with spotted hippo, even though she knew they'd be drinking water or fermented curds because that's all they had.

"What did you think of that Mr Thompkinson being split into two then, Mum?" asked Ruff.

"Serves him right," she said, which cheered her up. At least that common little man wouldn't ever be drinking wine again. Or water or curds for that matter.

Urgum grinned as he happily polished his axe.

"I don't mind admitting," he said to Divina. "I've been wrong all along about money. It's fantastic. Look at this brilliant fight we're going to have over half a tanna. Just think what a bag full of gold pieces could have started!"

Mungoid wasn't listening. He and Grizelda were both staring silently into the fire, but he was trying to judge whether she was sitting bolt upright, or could it be that she was leaning his way just ever so slightly? If only he could be sure that she was leaning his way

then maybe he'd dare himself to slip his arm around her shoulders...

PFARRRTUMMMMP!

The little trumpet pipe in the corner of the lounge tooted. Everybody dashed through to get it, leaving Grizelda and a very disappointed Mungoid together for a moment.

"Remember where you got to," Grizelda said to Mungoid as she stood up. "And next time start from there otherwise you and me will never get anywhere."

Twink, plink and dinkety-dink, Mungoid's three hairs shot up and did a little excited dance. Grizelda walked through into the lounge followed by Mungoid who floated through on a little cloud of joy.

When they got there Ruinn's voice was calling from the trumpet tube, "Wow! This is it! They're coming, battle engines and everything. Hundreds of them!"

"Are we going to take them all on?" Molly asked Urgum.

"It all depends," said Urgum. "How long is it before tea's ready?"

"About another three days," said Robbin who was holding a bucket of gravy under his arm and stirring it.

"Three days? Hundreds of them?" Urgum's head nearly exploded. Having to think about one number was bad enough, but thinking about two at once was asking for trouble. "What do you think, Mungoid? Have we time?"

"Absolutely yes!" Mungoid rubbed his hands together. "A little scrap before tea is just the thing to build up an appetite."

"Hundreds is a very big number, Urgum," said Divina. "I hope you've got some sort of plan."

"Well we don't shake hands with them." He grinned and for once he didn't care when Divina's angry eyebrow shot up.

He set out the plan to defend the cragg. The boys would go up to the ledge and prepare to drop more spiked boulders and totally scablitterize anyone passing underneath. Grizelda would be on the watchtower looking out for any officers among the army. Her job was to take them out quickly, leaving the forces in complete disarray. Mungoid would take position on Olk's right side, wearing his battle teeth.

"Do you want to stay back in the cave, dear?" Urgum asked Divina, whose eyebrow still hadn't gone down from last time.

"I do not," she snapped. "I shall prepare myself and take my place at Olk's other side." She stormed back into the kitchen.

"I bet she's gone to get the red-hot meat spit out of the fire!" said Molly excitedly.

"Or the long curved gutting knife." Robbin shuddered. "Imagine having that rammed down your throat and twisted round."

"Urghhh!" agreed everybody. Maybe their mum was going for the most gruesome death of the year prize?

But then Divina came out of the kitchen again, and she wasn't carrying a meat spit or a gutting knife. She was carrying a very large tray full of dainty party nibbles.

"Are you MAD?" asked Urgum.

"I don't care how rude or rough they are," said Divina, "they are from the palace and they are our visitors. And if they don't behave properly, I shall embarrass them to death."

"But you'll be slaughtered!"

"Nonsense," replied Divina. "Nobody ever slaughtered anybody who was offering them a sausage roll with mushroom dip."

Soon everybody had gone out to take up their positions, and only Urgum and Molly were left in the cave.

"You haven't said what you're doing, Dad," said Molly.

"I've got a special plan for me," said Urgum. He put on his hat, picked up his axe and a razor chain then walked through one of the archways at the back of the lounge.

"What plan?" asked Molly. She clutched a burning torch and followed him down the dark corridor. Surely he wasn't going to bed?

Urgum paused outside the entance to the toilet.

"This tax nonsense has to finish some time," said Urgum. "So it may as well be today. That's why I'm going to get them from behind. If any try to retreat, I'll have them. If we let them get away, they'll only come back."

"But how will you get round the back without them seeing?" said Molly.

"Thanks to Hunjah's building skills, there's a secret way out." Urgum grinned. "Look!" He stepped into the toilet cavelet and pointed at the hole in the floor. "I've got my axe and my razor chain, so that should do. That horse is out there somewhere, so as soon as I find it I'll be ready."

"Doesn't it scare you facing an army on your own?" said Molly.

"What's to be scared of?" asked Urgum.

"Death!" Molly said anxiously.

"Pah! That's not scary. Although now you mention it, if anything does happen to me, make sure you look after your mum. The desert needs her. After all, you don't get many people who go out to face an enemy army just armed with a tray of sausage rolls. "

"Of course, Dad," said Molly. "But I'll find out who killed you too, trust me."

"Good for you!" said Urgum. "If necessary, you track them down, hunt them out, doesn't matter how long or hard you have to look, just swear to me you'll find them."

"And then I'll kill them," said Molly.

"NO!" said Urgum. "What would you want to do that for? No, if you find the person that kills me, make sure they get my axe, and pass on my best wishes. I want that axe to go to someone worthy of it, and the only person worthy of it will be the person who can kill me in combat. Promise?"

"Promise..." said Molly uncertainly. "Well, goodbye then."

"Goodbye Molly," said Urgum.

Molly looked at her father, wondering if this was going to be the very last time she saw him alive. Just in case it was, she wanted to hold her final vision of him in her mind for ever.

And then Urgum jumped down the toilet.

Divine Breath

Molly walked back through the cave, not knowing what to think. If she had listened to Urgum's advice and not tried earning a few silly coins, none of this would have happened, and he wouldn't be planning to wipe out an army on his own. But then again, that's what he wanted to do and he was quite happy about it, even if it killed him.

She knew that she had to be brave and that it was her father's destiny to die in battle, but did it have to be now? It seemed like she'd only just met him and they still had such a lot to do together. He had to teach her how to be a true barbarian, and she ... well, if nothing else, she had to teach him what came after the letter "U" in "Urgum". Molly saw the copy of *Modern Savage* magazine lying on the shelf and she wiped away a tear as she remembered the joy with which he'd shown it to the tax collector. She picked it up and with trembling fingers she flicked through to check if the page where he'd found his letter "U" was as bad as she remembered it. To her utter astonishment she found herself looking at a fantastic feature entitled "Urgum, the Legend of the Lost Desert" with a rather good picture of her father holding his axe.

"Am I going mad?" she said to the two exhausted-looking little statues on the shelf. She'd seen them before, but had never paid much attention to them, although she knew Urgum liked them a lot. "Yes, I must be mad," she decided. "I'm talking to two little god statues now! Pity you're only models, maybe if you were real you could sort this mess out. I know we've all got to die some time, but can't I have just a bit more time with him? It's all so unfair."

Then, biting her lip to control her tears, Molly hurried away from the cave. She didn't want to go and stand on the ledge with the others in case they saw how worried she was, so she headed up to the watchtower to join Grizelda. Grizelda wouldn't laugh at her or ask awkward questions. In fact, if Molly couldn't learn to be a barbarian like Urgum, then learning to be a grisly like Grizelda was the next best thing.

It wasn't until Molly was safely out of sight that the eyes on the statues flickered into life once more. Both of them let out long tired sighs and sat themselves down on the shelf.

"What's her problem?" Tangor groaned. "Urgum will be all right. It's only a ragbag army of accountants."

"There's an awful lot of them," said Tangal. "And they are well armed. They might get lucky."

"So what can we do about it?" said Tangor, massaging his neck. "Moving all those trillions of ink atoms has worn me out."

"You know if Urgum dies, he'll be at our table eating for ever."

"We'll just have to risk it." Tangor sighed. "I'm utterly whacked."

"But think what might happen to Molly," said Tangal, shuffling over to the edge of the shelf and then letting her feet dangle down in mid-air. "We put her here and we have a duty to look after her."

"Oh," said Tangor. "I never thought of that."

"Remember what she said," said Tangal. "If we were real we could sort this mess out! Well, if we did sort it out, she might start believing in us. Let's face it, we could do with a few more true believers."

"So what do we do?" asked Tangor. "We could set up an earthquake or an avalache or a shower of cobras or something."

"It can't be anything too big," said Tangal. "The tax gods would be on us like a flash. We'd never hear the end of it if we stopped a legitimate bit of tax collecting."

"Legitimate?" muttered Tangor, getting an idea. "That's it! We've all forgotten something important. Come on, we can stop this if we hurry."

Once again the little statues fell dormant, but at the same instant, many miles away, there was a sudden chill in Laplace Palace where the dizzalid was marching around the abandoned offices of her tax department in a fury. Every desk and chair was empty and her temper was not improved when she found the explanation pinned to the noticeboard in the form of an F28. The whole of her department had been deployed to collect an outstanding payment of ... *half a bronze tanna*. The dizzalid knew it was ridiculous, but it was the law and there was nothing she could do. Angrily she slumped into her own chair and tossed her record book on to her desk, but as she drummed her claws beside it a sharp breeze flipped the book open.

She slammed it shut again, but the breeze seemed to return and once more opened it up. She watched, mesmerized, as the pages riffled over, but then a second breeze came in from the other side and started riffling the pages back. Back and forth the pages flipped and slapped more and more frantically as if some invisible person or persons were looking for something.

And then, as suddenly as the disturbance had started, it stopped and all was silent. The dizzalid cast an eye down to the open page. Seconds later, she had scooped up the book and was rushing out to her horse, her long tail thrashing wildly behind her.

The two breezes sighed in relief.

"I thought we'd never find it!" Tangor gasped.

"Me too," agreed Tangal. "Let's just hope that we were in time."

It's Showtime

As the troops amassed outside the mouthway to the cragg, Mungoid went to stand beside Olk. He had come prepared for business, his new battle teeth were securely fixed in and he was carrying his monstrous metal Ungoid battle-mallet. In front of them, the whole tax army had assembled. The little tax collector worked his way to the front.

"It'th pwobably better ifth you leth me do the thalking," said Mungoid through his big teeth.

On Olk's other side, Divina raised her eyebrow. She was not convinced that Mungoid's talking was going to help anybody while he had those teeth in. Nevertheless she just flicked a fly off one of the duck paté vol-au-vents on her tray and said nothing.

"Coo-ee, anyone home?" Mr Perkins said sarcastically as he looked at everybody in their positions around the cragg. Behind him the troops all laughed.

"Hello again Mr Perkins," said Divina brightly.

"Perhaps I could tempt a few of your colleagues to a nibble?"

"Mmmm!" An appreciative noise came from the army.

"Shut up!" ordered the collector. "We are not playing games any more. We're coming in."

"Password," said Olk.

"I think we've got past that point," said the collector. "It's time you met Miss Blenkinsop from the Invoice Filing Department."

"You'll forgive me if I don't shake hands," said Divina dryly.

From the middle of the troops came a clanking, grinding sound. The horses at the front stepped aside and two massive oxen dragged a huge cannon into place. A small woman in huge boots was sitting astride it and under her supervision the barrel was carefully aimed directly at Olk's chest. In her hands she held a pieced of tarred rope and a spark flint.

"Are you already loaded, Miss Blenkinsop?" asked the collector.

Miss Blenkinsop nodded then, hopping down from the cannon, she took up her position by the small fire nozzle at the far end.

"It's your last chance," said Mr Perkins. "Either fatty clears out of the way or Miss Blenkinsop will blast a hole right through him."

"Wow, imagine that!" exclaimed Ruinn, high above. "If you crawled through it you could see all Olk's insides pumping away around you."

"It's sure to kill him," said Ruff. "He'll have to move aside."

"Olk won't move," said Robbin. "He's got his pride, you know."

The collector grinned. "Prepare to fire, Miss Blenkinsop!"

As Miss Blenkinsop struck a flint spark and lit the piece of tarred rope, Mungoid briefly rested his

hammer on the ground and spat on his hands.

Grabbing the handle again, he swung the heavy head up on to his shoulder then went to stand directly between Olk and the cannon.

"Get out of the way!" snapped Mr Perkins.

"Actually I thuggetht thath you thell thoth riderth of yourth over thowardth the alley to thift over to one thide," said Mungoid.

"Didn't understand a word of that," said the collector.

"That'th thoo bad for them then," said Mungoid.

"FIRE!" shouted Mr Perkins.

Miss Blenkinsop put the burning rope to the fire hole of the cannon and...

BOOM - ZACKLANGG - WHOOSH - SPLATT - "URGHHH" - "HURRAH!!"

The ball shot from the cannon, Mungoid swung his great hammer round and smacked it straight at Smiley Alley where it knocked over several palace horsemen like a row of skittles. From above, the boys all cheered like mad.

"AWESOME!" they shouted.

"But does it beat Olk for gruesome death?" asked Robbin.

"It *was* good!" admitted Ruinn. "Oh yes indeedy, that was very good."

But best of all a piercing wolf-whistle came from the watchtower and when Mungoid looked up he saw Molly leaping up and down cheering ... and so was Grizelda! Mungoid was so elated that it was quite some time before he became aware of a deep purring sound that he'd never heard before.

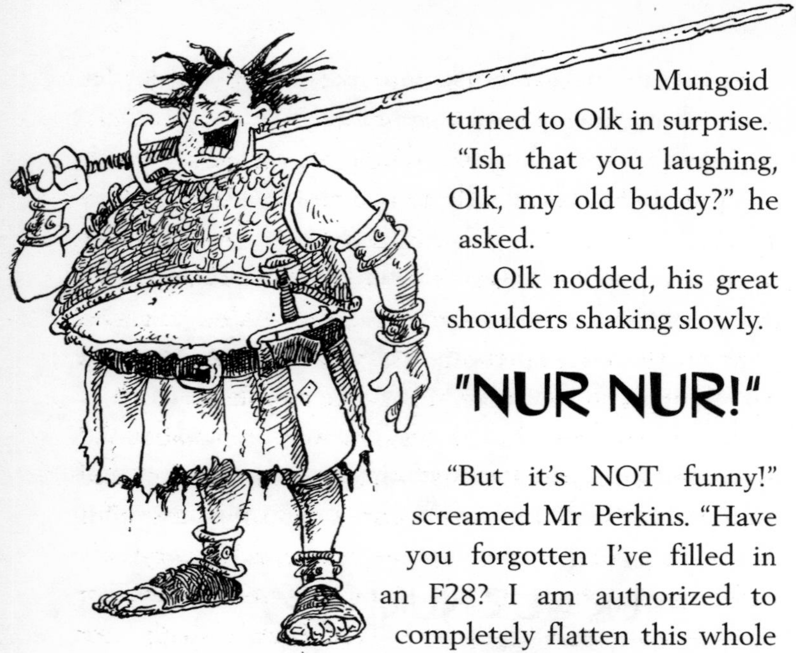

Mungoid turned to Olk in surprise. "Ish that you laughing, Olk, my old buddy?" he asked.

Olk nodded, his great shoulders shaking slowly.

"NUR NUR!"

"But it's NOT funny!" screamed Mr Perkins. "Have you forgotten I've filled in an F28? I am authorized to completely flatten this whole cragg with all of you in it. I have archers, small fire, spears and javelins all trained at this gateway. You can't hope to withstand them all, and when you're finished, I have a squadron of mounted lancers to cut you down and break inside."

"Then the time for thpeecheth ith over," muttered Mungoid. "Thith ith it."

"But before we start," said Divina. "Who'd like a liver and pineapple chunk?"

She had no takers, because the entire army was poised for attack. Bowstrings were back, swords were out, spears were up and the whole plain held its breath ready for the bloodbath that would surely follow. Mungoid's eyes flitted back and forth, his knuckles white around the handle of his hammer. High above the plain the boys had every single boulder balanced right on the edge of the ledge, and overhead the two very happy vultures were licking their beaks.

A cold silence fell: the tension was unbearable. All eyes were on Mr Perkins who braced himself and prepared to issue the biggest command of his life. This was his big moment, he was in charge, and everybody had to respect him and him alone, and he was loving it and he wanted it to last for ever. Well actually, not *everybody* was respecting him...

"NUR NUR NUR!"

"That's it!" snapped the collector, his eyes almost bursting from his head, furious at having his big moment ruined. He raised a long mace. "I was going to give you one last chance, but you've blown it. When I lower this mace, you're dead. ALL of you. Three, two, one..."

SSSSTH-WAK!

"...ARGHH!"

One of Grizelda's orange-flighted arrows had gone through the back of his hand and the mace fell to the ground.

"Arghh?" whispered all the troops. "Did he say 'arghhh'? I thought he was going to say 'attack'."

"And did he really lower the mace? Does dropping it count?"

"I dunno."

Just then Molly appeared by Divina's side, breathless from running.

"The dizzalid's coming!" she shouted. "Grizelda and me just saw her from the watchtower."

There was an uncertain muttering in the troops as they all looked round to watch the white-haired lizard woman on her horse galloping past the fallen riders by Smiley Alley and on towards the cragg wall.

"Attack anyway," screamed Mr Perkins, waving his

bloody hand with the arrow sticking from it. "Go on, do it. Let them have it!"

But nobody was listening to him any more. The dizzalid pulled her sweating horse up in front of Divina.

"Retract your positions," the dizzalid ordered the territorials in her low, powerful voice. "And hold fire."

The dizzalid rode up to the collector who had just yanked the arrow out of his hand with his teeth.

"Who authorized the F28?"

"Me!" He yelped, letting the arrow drop to the ground. "Debt outstanding and refusal to pay."

"There was no debt."

"But they owe half a tanna!" said the collector wrapping a handkerchief around his bleeding hand. "It's been an ongoing uncooperative situation for months."

"Check the paperwork," said the dizzalid slapping her boring book across his face. "They were half a tanna in credit."

"Eh?" said everybody at once.

The dizzalid spoke to Molly.

"When I first called, you paid four tannas but you only owed three and a half," she explained. "So you had half a tanna in credit. It's all listed here, if only *somebody* had taken the trouble to look."

"So you mean..." began the collector, "...all this...?"

"A little heavy handed, wouldn't you say?" said the dizzalid coldly.

"But but..." said the collector.

"From now you are on official reprimand," said the dizzalid. "And to these fair-minded, law-abiding people, you owe an apology."

"Apologize? To savages? Never! I am an important offical of the palace..."

"Or shall I leave you with them? I'm sure they have ways to make you feel very sorry."

"Ho ho!" said Mungoid. "I darethay we could think of something."

"NUR NUR NUR!"

"No!" bleated the collector. "You can't leave me here. You are my superior and therefore responsible for my welfare."

"Not if I sack you, you're not," said the dizzalid.

"You can't sack me!" said the collector. "If you try I'll just fill in form ND 19c against unfair dismissal, and if that fails I'll go to appeal. "

The dizzalid's black tongue shot out and lashed across her face in frustration, but then to everybody's surprise Molly stepped forwards.

"I think Mr Perkins has done a wonderful job," said Molly.

"Eh?" They all gasped.

"See?" said the collector.

"If it wasn't for him I'd never have understood the tax system and I would have been living my life as an unwitting criminal not knowing that I owed money to the State."

"You've been out in the sun too long," muttered Divina.

"No really," said Molly. "In fact now everything's settled, I'd like to offer you dinner."

"Me? Dinner?"

"Yes, I've a friend who has a little restaurant out by the crossroads. You'll see the entrance if you ride down Smiley Alley, and listen out for the music. Just pop in and say Molly sent you."

"Really?"

"Oh yes," said Molly. "I'm sure he'd be glad to er ... have you in for dinner."

Everybody looked at Molly in amazement but she

just smiled at the collector and waved him away.

"Go on then!" she said. "What are you waiting for?"

The collector immediately rode off. Up above on the ledge Robbin smirked.

"What's so funny?" asked Ruinn.

"Trust me." Robbin laughed. "If there's a prize for gruesome death of the year, then Molly just won it!"

Down below, Divina offered her tray to the dizzalid.

"I'm sorry I haven't any scorpions," said Divina.

"And I'm sorry things got a bit out of hand," said the dizzalid.

The dizzalid looked up at the row of spiked boulders, then across at the watchtower where Grizelda still had her bow raised. Glancing back down she took in Olk's blade and Mungoid's battle teeth. She gave a little shiver of relief.

"It seems I got here just in time," she said.

Gradually, Grizelda lowered her bow, Mungoid removed his battle teeth, the boys stood back from the boulders. Everyone relaxed and a few of the territorials even wandered forward to take up Divina's offer of nibbles.

"That's better." Divina smiled contentedly. "Everybody's being very nice and nobody is getting seriously hurt."

And that's when from the back of the assembled troops they heard the wildest blood-crazed scream...

"YARGGGGGGHHHH...

The Last Charge

...HHHHHHH!"

It had been a long time since Urgum had slid to the end of the toilet drain and clambered out of the hole and down the cliff. He had found his horse and after a bit of an argument he'd got on it and waited out of sight round the back of the cragg. He'd been listening out for the big fight to start but after a while started to worry that everything was too quiet and wondered if their defences had all gone badly wrong. Maybe those idiot sons of his had dropped the spiked boulders on to Olk and Mungoid? Maybe an archer had got lucky and taken out Grizelda before she'd had a chance to fire? Maybe ... maybe the collectors had got inside and were ransacking his cave and taking Molly and Divina captive?

That's why, with his axe in one hand and a weighted razor chain in the other, Urgum spurred his horse forward. From the shadow of the rock behind the troops, he emerged screaming with all his joyous might.

"AM I SCARED?

NO!

DO I CARE?

NO!

I'M COMPLETELY

MENTAL!"

The nearest soldiers had their backs towards him and, as word had already reached them about Divina offering round party snacks, they had lowered their shields and put away their swords. On hearing the barbarian battle cry, they tried to turn round and draw their swords again, but too late. One or two at the edge of the army managed to gallop out of the way, but the rest of the force was too tightly packed to move into position to face him.

TRUN-DUDDLE-UN-DUDDLE-UN-DUDDLE-UN...

As Urgum's horse ploughed forwards straight into the thickest part of the crowd, Urgum spared a second to admire his great beast. True, it was an antisocial disobedient old nag most of the time, but when it came to a good fight, the horse knew it had to show full respect to its master and do its duty fearlessly. *Good old horse,* thought Urgum.

TRUN-DUDDLE-UN-DUDDLE-UN-DUDDLE-UN...

Stupid old fat bloke, thought the horse as it charged. The horse knew that people generally liked horses and didn't harm them if they could help it. It also knew that lots of people did not like Urgum, and so it took great satisfaction in delivering his overweight sweaty obnoxious rider into the middle of hostile armies. Keeping its head down, the horse barged its way through towards the roughest, toughest and meanest looking members of the tax territorials.

TRUN-DUDDLE-UN-DUDDLE-UN-DUDDLE-UN...

"Oh no!" wailed Divina as the screams of the injured and dying came from the back of the ranks. "It's Urgum. He doesn't know it's all sorted out!"

"Tell him to stop," ordered the dizzalid.

"STOP!" shouted the whole army at once.

"Ah shaddup!" screamed Urgum. "You should have thought of that before you all came here taking money from little girls."

By now some of the army had turned to fight, if only to save their own lives. All around him, the soldiers were trying to hack at Urgum with swords, daggers, spears and anything else they had with a metal spiky bit

on the end. Urgum was aware that he was being cut and stabbed at from all directions, and he even thought that he could feel something like a small stick tapping on his leg, but his barbarian instinct was to shut out all the pain and focus on despatching one enemy at a time. To his right, a mounted guard (Mr Peterson from Surcharge Levies) was lunging at him with a long curved sabre.

"YOU FIRST!" shouted Urgum and, with a hard swipe, his axe cut straight into the guard's shoulder –

SHTUNK

– and the arm fell to the ground. A few other weapons were making their marks on him (and he was sure he could feel that small stick tapping again), but Urgum's biggest threat was now coming from Mrs Patterson from Unauthorized Claims who had gashed his cheek with a spear. "NOW YOU!" he screamed as his weighted razor chain lashed out.

With a flick and a jerk it wrapped around Mrs Patterson's wrist and with one extra tug,

the hand fell to the ground.

"STOP STOP!" everyone shouted at him, but Urgum hadn't even started.

"It's too late to be sorry," screamed Urgum. "Who's next?"

A mallet slammed into his side shattering a few unimportant ribs. In reply, Urgum gave a mighty kick of his boot –

FADDUNK

– and the assailant (Mr Timms from the Interest Adjudication panel) was knocked to the ground where he was accidentally trampled by his own panicking horse. More blows rained down as Urgum drove, hacked and slashed his way forwards through the Tax Territorials, but it was all too easy for him. None of this inexperienced mob could damage the legendary barbarian enough to stop him. True, an arrow had thudded into his shoulder, a barbed dagger was dangling from a raw wound in his arm, blood was pouring from a series of gashes in his head, his tunic and trousers were drenched in crimson gore, but Urgum's biggest worry was that the silly little scars he'd pick up from this minor tiff would be laughed at.

BIFF CHOP WHAM SPLUDGE

He was almost falling asleep from boredom apart from just one little thing which was puzzling him. Whichever way he turned and whatever he did, he could still feel that small stick tapping on his leg and it was seriously starting to get on his nerves. Suddenly he could take it no more. Ignoring the flashing swords and daggers he looked down to see where it was coming from and there, crammed between all the sweating, bucking, blood-soaked horses, was one small foot soldier.

"Hello Urgum," said Mr Hunjah from Disposable Assets.

"Oh no!" wailed Urgum as he found himself looking into the face of the patheticest barbarian that ever lived. "What are you doing down there, Hunjah?"

"Well," said Hunjah, "it's quite a story actually. You see the building work wasn't really paying, so I took a temporary job as a filing clerk..."

"HUNJAH!"

screamed Urgum.

"I'M THE FIERCEST BARBARIAN THAT THE LOST DESERT HAS EVER KNOWN,

SO WILL YOU PLEASE STOP TAPPING ME WITH THAT FLIPPIN' STICK!"

"But I failed my sword exam, and I get horsesick when I'm riding," explained Hunjah, "so this is all I'm allowed."

Urgum was so utterly speechless at the patheticness of Hunjah that for a moment he completely forgot what he was supposed to be doing, and that's when Mr Headnappar (the tax department's newest, tallest and filthiest recruit) took his chance. Up until this moment the lanky bandit had kept his head ducked down behind his horse's neck so that Urgum wouldn't notice his distinctive snot-coloured hair, but on seeing that the barbarian was distracted he sat up and drew a long jagged sabre. Rearing his horse on to its back legs behind Urgum, he stretched his arms right up, grasping the weapon in both hands.

"I've been waiting a long time for this," screeched the headnappar, but just as he was plunging the blade into the side of Urgum's neck, an orange-flighted arrow appeared, sticking from his eye socket. The nappar tumbled to the ground dead before he could scream, but the damage was already done. A fountain of blood shot out to indicate that, at last, the barbarian had taken a major strike. Urgum immediately knew this was serious, and he also knew exactly whose fault it was.

"Hunjah, you little wart!" He clasped his hand to the spurting wound. "This is your fault for putting me off!"

"Don't blame me," said Hunjah. "You're the one that asked me what I was doing here. Anyway, once I'd qualified as a filing clerk..."

Urgum just couldn't take any more. With one hand still clamped over his neck, he reached down with the other, grabbed Hunjah's head, lifted it clear of his shoulders and screamed into his face,

"HUNJAH WILL YOU SHUT UP??!"

"There's no need to be like that." Hunjah sniffed. "After all, you did ask..."

Suddenly the blows and bashes stopped as all around

them the Tax Territorial Army realized that Urgum was having a conversation with a severed head which was answering back.

"SHUT UP SHUT UP!"

pleaded Urgum, slumping forward on his horse as the world around him started to spin.

"Now you've got everybody looking," said Hunjah's head.

"SHUT UP!"

"All right, I'll shut up if you put my head back!" said Hunjah. "You see, I didn't want anyone to know in case I failed the fitness test."

"YARGHHHHH!"

screamed Urgum, dropping the head on the ground. As Hunjah's body groped its way over to find it, the retreat stampede started. Horses, riders, soldiers, cannons, archers

– the whole area was a mass panic as the utterly horrified Tax Territorial Army tripped and trampled over itself struggling to get away. Running after them was Mr Hunjah from Disposable Assets, trying to hold his head steady on his shoulders.

Soon just Urgum was left sitting on his horse, one hand clutching his neck, the other swinging his axe madly around his head. He was unable to see that he was all alone because of the blood caked over his face.

"YARGHHHH!

Let's have you!" he was screaming. "Bring on your best!"

The horse did a bored snort and looked over at the dizzalid who was standing alongside Divina, Mungoid, Olk and Molly. Every single one of them had their mouths hanging open in utter disbelief.

"YARGHHHH!

You robbers of children! You softhand snot heads! Where are you? The only way you'll kill me is if I die of boredom waiting."

The horse sighed, then spotted a nice clump of unbloodied grass just by its front feet. *Why not?* the horse thought, and it reached down to eat it. After all, he knew that when Urgum was in this mood it could last for hours.

"What's the matter with him?" Molly asked Mungoid.

"He's gone berserk," said Mungoid. "And it's a bad

one. Best to keep your distance."

"But how long will it last?" asked Molly.

"Until it stops," said Mungoid.

"I want it to stop now!" Molly broke away from the group and hurried towards her father.

"Molly!" cried Mungoid. "NO!" He dashed forward to grab her, but she nimbly evaded his grasp.

"Molly, he'll kill anyone in this mood!"

But Molly wasn't going to turn back. Stepping over the bits of injured tax officials she approached the berserk barbarian.

"YARGHHHH!"

cried Urgum. "I'm completely mental!"

"Dad!" shouted Molly. "Stop! It's all over."

"YARGHHHH!"

"STOP DAD!" screamed Molly. "STOP!"

"YARGHH!"

"Stop now!"

"YAR?"

"Stoppit."

"Molly?" said Urgum. "Is that you?"

"It's me," said Molly. "Now stop."

Slowly Urgum lowered his arm. The dripping axe fell from his grasp and clattered to the ground.

"I can't see you," he said. "Am I dead?"

"Not yet, Dad," said Molly, trying to stop her voice from trembling. "But if you don't let us patch you up, you soon will be."

As Urgum's berserk rage subsided, the pain from his wounds and broken bones suddenly started to take hold. He put his hand in his mouth and bit down on it hard to try and prevent himself from screaming. He was desperate not to let his little girl see that her father could feel pain just as much as any other common mortal.

"Dad?" asked Molly. "Dad, are you OK?"

Up in the watchtower, Grizelda knew exactly what what going on and raised her bow.

Suddenly there was an arrow sticking out of Urgum's breastplate. It was a very slim arrow that shone in the sunlight. The pin-sharp tip wasn't wide enough to cause physical damage, but the trace of liquid coating had its effect. The chaos-spider venom seeped into Urgum's bloodstream and soon reached his brain. Once there it formed a mesh of haemoglobic webs slowing down the thought processes and bringing his entire nervous system to a halt.

As Urgum fell from his saddle, Mungoid dashed forward to catch him.

"Dad!" cried Molly. "Dad?"

"Let him rest," explained Mungoid, as he laid his friend on the ground. "Grizelda's just put him to sleep. It's the only chance he's got of getting through this."

Over by the cragg entrance, the dizzalid murmured to Divina, "I've never seen anyone fight like that. Ever."

"He's killed a lot of your people," said Divina.

"We were at fault," said the dizzalid simply. "I'll see you get a compensation claim form."

"I don't want compensation," snapped Divina. "I want my husband."

"I don't blame you," said the dizzalid. "If he was mine, so would I."

Mungoid had gently laid Urgum out on the ground and was kneeling beside him. Molly was standing by his shoulder.

"He's taken a terrible amount of damage," said Mungoid softly.

"Will he get better?"

"Maybe, maybe not," said Mungoid sadly, but then, clearing his throat, he tried to sound brighter. "But don't worry about him. He was fighting to defend his family with honour, courage and absolutely no common sense whatsoever. He will have pleased his gods and soon he'll be up there feasting at their table for eternity. He'll be happy."

"I don't want him with the gods!" Molly wept.

"I want him here with me!"

"Of course you do," said Mungoid. He wiped some of the gory mess away from his friend's face. Blood had stopped pumping from the neck wound but Urgum's eyelids were closed and his breathing kept starting and stopping in little awkward jerks. "But for that he's going to need help. An awful lot of help."

Divina came over and stood silently beside Molly with her hand on her daughter's shoulder. "What can we do, Mungoid?"

Mungoid swallowed. His huge ugly face looked strangely soft and deflated as he straightened Urgum's hat.

"Turn up the heat on that spotted hippo," he replied.

Divina's eyebrow shot up furiously, but Mungoid wasn't joking.

"Old Urgum and me have been mates for just about ever," he explained. "And believe me, there's only one thing we can do if we're to have the slightest chance of saving him."

With the back of his hand he wiped away the tears that were dripping off the end of his great nose, then looked straight at Molly.

"We're going to have to throw a really really massive mummy-hugging monster of a party."

The Deliverance

It was deep into the night and the torch in Urgum's bedroom was burning low. The barbarian was lying flat out on the four-poster bed with his arms folded across his chest, hugging his great axe. His eyes were closed and his breath was coming in short uncomfortable bursts. Beside him on a low stool sat an anxious little girl taking a long look at her father. Those ox-like shoulders, the leathery skin, the heavy-boned skull, the rippling muscles – even when he was unconscious Urgum was an awesome sight. But Molly had been sitting there so long that, even though she hated to admit it, he had became a very boring awesome sight.

Through the doorway came the faint echo of heavy drums being beaten away out in the main part of Golgarth basin, accompanied by a few cheers, laughs, the odd scream and the smell of almost perfectly burnt spotted hippo. Occasionally the noise and smells were enough to disturb Urgum and he would shift slightly, but then he would slip off into unconsciousness again.

In the bedroom, two small flames detached themselves from the torch on the wall and floated over to examine Urgum. Molly just thought they were moths and paid them no attention.

Tangor's face shimmered in the first flame. "What's happened to him?" he said. "He's supposed to be a wild and reckless savage. He should have dragged himself to that party! He can't just lie there dying, he should be out there behaving disgracefully."

"He'll be all right." Tangal shimmered in the second flame, trying to sound confident. "We've stopped the worst of the bleeding. All he has to do is get up on his feet."

"But what if he doesn't want to?" asked Tangor, as his flame flitted past the closed eyelids. "Maybe he's hurt so badly that he's decided to die and join us and eat for eternity. Of course this is all your fault."

"MY fault?" said Tangal.

"You sent down Molly!"

"Molly was a good idea!" said Tangal. "She was a harmless joke to make him settle down and stop him risking his life in stupid ways."

"Well the joke went wrong, didn't it?" said Tangor. "Thanks to Molly, his last two fights were started by a squashed flower and half a tanna and now he's dying. You can't get much stupider than that."

"Don't blame Molly!" said Tangal. "In fact, if anyone can get him on his feet again, she can. Mungoid and Divina know that, it's why they left her to watch him."

"What's the point?" Tangor sighed. "We always knew we had to lose our last true barbarian sometime. And when there's no one left alive to believe in us, then we're finished too."

But then his sister's little flame-face glowed with a bright golden thought. Tangal shot over behind Molly and flitted around excitedly.

"We're not finished yet!" she cried. "Urgum could train up a new barbarian for us. It would involve him showing off all his skills and experience, and he'd love that! Showing off is one of his favourite things."

"Nice thought," said Tangor. "But who's he going to

train? Those sons will never be true barbarians. They haven't got the right respect or the right attitude."

"I'm not talking about the sons!" Tangal formed a circle of fire around Molly's head. (It's a pity Molly didn't see it because it looked really ace.) "I mean the daughter."

"Molly?" Tangor gasped. "Of course – she's got respect, she's certainly got attitude and she's scared of nothing."

"He could make her into a great barbarian," said Tangal, "if only he'd get moving again."

Tangor's flame shot round to whisper in Urgum's ear. "Come on Urgum. "Wake up, you've got some showing off to do. Well? You know you like showing off!"

Although a small smile crossed Urgum's lips, he didn't move.

"No good?" said Tangal. Her flame circle shrunk back

down to a sad flicker. "If only there was something to kick his brain into activity. Anything at all..."

"Hang on!" said Tangor. "It was fighting for Molly's money that finished him..."

"Don't try to blame me again!"

"No, listen," insisted Tangor, "he never even saw the present she bought him, did he?"

The two flames suddenly burst with hopeful sparks.

"That's it!" exclaimed Tangal. "Apart from showing off and eating, what's the other most lovable quality about our last true barbarian?"

"GREED!" they both shouted.

Urgum's breathing had been getting fainter and fainter and then at that moment his arms slackened and the axe started to slip from his grasp. Tangal hurriedly flitted over to whisper in Molly's ear. Of course, Molly didn't really hear what the flame said but she suddenly realized that there was something that she desperately wanted to do.

She rose to her feet and just before the axe handle reached the floor, she grabbed it, but rather than trying to replace the axe on her father's chest, she gently tried to ease it away. It was very heavy, and Urgum's hands were still holding the axe head in a feeble grip. She pulled a bit harder and then with a solid

CLUNG

the metal head slipped free and fell down to hit the floor of the cave. Tangor's little flame had ducked below Urgum's earlobe and was burning just enough to cause one very tired bloodshot eye to flicker open and watch Molly dragging the axe over to the corner of the cave.

"Wassat?" muttered Urgum, but so softly Molly didn't hear him. Slowly Urgum's other eye opened and he even turned his head to get a better view – the girl seemed to be trying to lift the axe head up against the cave wall. It made no sense and didn't seem worth the effort. Urgum was about to drift back into his unconscious state again so, in desperation, Tangor's flame glowed white hot for an instant.

"EEK!" Urgum yelped, shaking his head and surprising Molly so much that she lost her grip. The heavy axe fell to the floor with another

CLUNG!

"What's that noise?" Urgum groaned. "Stop it. There's people trying to die here."

"Dad!" cried Molly. "You're alive!"

"No I'm not," muttered Urgum, lowering his head back down on to the bed. "I'm dead. Now give me my axe back and let me get on with it."

"No way!" said Molly. "You're not allowed to die. You've got to be at the party."

"Party?" mumbled Urgum. "What party?"

"A really really massive mummy-hugging monster of a party," said Molly. "Mungoid's fixing it. There's axe tossing, fire belching, bear mauling and Mum's even doing a special recipe for that spotted hippo. Can't you smell it?"

Urgum's nose sniffed deeply and got so excited that it started twitching and trembling as if it had already arrived at the party and was having a dance by itself.

"Come on, Dad!" Molly grabbed his hand and pulled as hard as she could. "It's going to be great."

"Well of course it'll be great!" Urgum snatched his hand from her grip. "Mungoid always did great parties, but why now? I'm dying in great agony here! Doesn't anyone care? People shouldn't be having parties, they should be being sad and standing round saying what a super bloke I was."

"Super?" Molly sneered. "You? Lying there bleating about a bit of pain instead of going to a party? And you call yourself a barbarian. Honestly, I wish I hadn't got you that present now."

"Present? For me? What present?"

"I'll only tell you if you get up," said Molly. "Go on, get up!"

Molly tugged on his hand again and very slowly Urgum raised himself to a sitting position. He had to lean on his arms to prop himself up, but once he'd stopped swaying, Molly skipped across the cave and pointed at something on the wall. Urgum peered across and saw it was a large double hook made of solid brass.

"What's that?" he said.

"It's a special axe hook for hanging axes on," said Molly. She reached down for the axe and tried to heave it up but still she couldn't quite lift it on to the hook.

CLUNG

– it hit the floor again.

"It fits, honest," said Molly. "I just can't get it on."

"Oh," said Urgum and promptly laid back down again.

"It'll stop you chopping your toes in half," said Molly crossly. "I got it for you with my money and it cost five tannas, so say you like it."

Urgum sighed. "I liked my other present better." Slowly he moved his hand up to his neck, then reached inside his shirt and pulled out his little flower necklace.

"The flower necklace?" Molly gasped. "You still wear it?"

"Remember what you said when you gave it to me?" asked Urgum. As tired as he was, he still managed to raise a proud smile. "My dad's not scared to wear a flower necklace, because he's the toughest dad in the world."

"Huh!" snapped Molly. "I'd never have given you it if I'd known you were just going to roll over and die on me."

"It's my destiny," said Urgum pompously. "I have lived a full and glorious life, and now the time has come for me to meet my grateful gods."

"Why are you so keen to meet them?" said Molly. "You don't even know what they're like."

"Yes I do," retorted Urgum. "They are marvellous strong noble beings, pretty much like myself, I expect."

The twin gods exchanged embarrassed glances. It was a good job Urgum couldn't see the two little flames trying to hide down in the corner and being turned green by the smelly draught coming from the toilet next door.

"I'll probably end up being a god myself," he continued. "You see, Molly, you are looking at the last of the true barbarians."

"No I'm not," said Molly defiantly. "You are."

"Eh?" replied Urgum. "The only person I'm looking at is you!"

"Yes, and I'm going to be a true barbarian. I've been watching my brothers warm up for the party games. They can teach me all I need."

"That lot? Hah!" Urgum snorted. "You'll be lucky. There's not a barbaric bone between them. They simply haven't got it."

"Ruinn has been tossing axes, he's really good. He's going to teach me how one day."

"Ruinn? He couldn't toss a stick at the ground. Don't listen to him."

"The twins are going to show me fire belching."

"Huh! Those two would choke on a candle flame."

"Robbin is going to show me how to maul bears."

"Robbin? Maul bears? Oh, I suppose he's got the moves," admitted Urgum, "but he's got no technique. He can only take on two at once. And as for you, well just look at you! How are you EVER going to maul a bear?"

Molly could stand for it no more.

"If you're QUITE finished then I've got news for you," she said furiously. "Maybe I'm not as big or as strong OR as smelly as you, but I'll still be a better barbarian than you AND do you know why? Because when I die it won't be because I'm feeling too SORRY FOR MYSELF to get to a party."

"What?"

"I mean it," she cried. "Go on, die. What does it matter to you if there's nobody to show me how things should really be done? I'll manage just fine without you."

Molly stomped off towards the door sulking massively. Her eyes glared in fury, her lower lip stuck out like a tongue. To her surprise Urgum burst out laughing, and even when it turned to a violent coughing fit he was still smiling.

"WHAT?" she demanded crossly.

"Come here," said Urgum when he had recovered his breath. He beckoned her over to sit on the bed next to where he was lying.

Molly reluctantly approached the end of the bed furthest away from him and sat down with a clumsy thud.

"Come here," insisted Urgum.

Molly shuffled herself a fraction closer, then folded her arms and stared at her knees.

"Er ... ahem." Urgum cleared his throat rather sheepishly. Although Molly's head didn't move her eyes briefly darted towards him. He was up to something but she didn't know what.

"Listen Molly," said Urgum. "I know this might seem stupid but..."

"It does seem stupid."

"Yeah, OK, it does," said Urgum. "But, well, I was just thinking: I never wanted a daughter, but I'm glad I've got you."

"Even though you think a weedy girl can't be a proper barbarian?"

"Like I said, I'm glad I've got you."

Molly's head turned towards Urgum, her eyes popped wide open, her mouth trembled in shock. After a moment she shook her head, flexed her shoulders and replied, "Yes, well if it comes to that, if I've got to have a father, then I'm glad I've got you. Even if you're fat and selfish."

She reached over and poked him in the ribs. And then before Molly knew it, Urgum had pushed himself upright and given her a very quick kiss on the forehead. Molly's heart nearly pounded its way out through her chest in instant rapture.

"What are you looking at?" asked Urgum trying to pretend that nothing exceptional had just happened.

"Nothing," said Molly staring at him as if a bunch of flowers had just shot out of his ear.

"So we've got each other then," said Urgum.

"Yes, Dad."

Then, slowly and painfully, Urgum swung his legs off the bed and staggered to his feet. Keeping one hand on the cave wall, he forced himself to take a few wobbly steps but then DUNK! He caught his toe on the axe blade, but luckily he didn't split it this time. Instead, he stumbled over towards Molly who quickly leapt up and pulled his great arm around her shoulders to keep him upright. Together they reached down for the mighty axe and with a great heave they managed to hoist it up on to the hook. Still leaning on Molly, Urgum took a step back and admired it.

"No more split toes." He sighed contentedly. "That is one very good present, Molly."

Then, still leaning on his daughter, he grabbed the burning torch from the wall. Neither of them noticed the two little flames flitting back up to join the rest of the blaze.

"What are you doing, Dad?"

"We've got work to do!" Urgum headed unsteadily towards the doorway.

"I thought you were off to meet your grateful gods," said Molly as they shuffled together down the corridor.

"They'll have to wait," hissed Urgum through gritted teeth. A few of his wounds had ripped open again and were feeling decidedly raw, but there was a defiant glint in his eyes as he ushered Molly into the lounge. "Come on! You and me have got to show those sad people how true barbarians party."

"You mean we're axe tossing and fire belching?" asked Molly excitedly.

"Yeah!" said Urgum, grateful for the stabs of pain which were waking him up more with every agonising step as they staggered towards the cave entrance.

"And even bear mauling?"

"Absolutely," said Urgum.

"Honest?" Molly gasped delightedly. "You really mean it? Me too?"

"What's the matter?" asked Urgum.

"ARE YOU SCARED?

NO!

DO YOU CARE?

NO!

WE'RE COMPLETELY

MENTAL!"

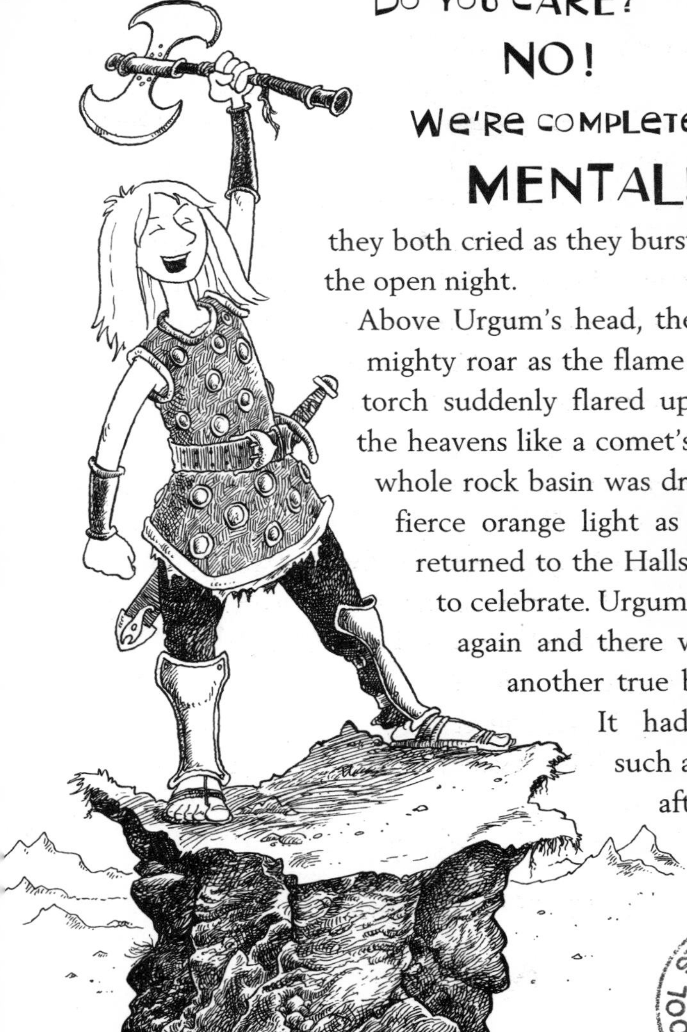

they both cried as they burst out into the open night.

Above Urgum's head, there was a mighty roar as the flame from the torch suddenly flared upwards to the heavens like a comet's tail. The whole rock basin was drowned in fierce orange light as the gods returned to the Halls of Sirrus to celebrate. Urgum was alive again and there was to be another true barbarian.

It hadn't been such a bad joke after all.

KJARTAN POSKITT

is the bestselling author of the *Murderous Maths* series and many other books, most of which were illustrated by Philip Reeve. He was born and lives in York and has a wife, four daughters and about 1300 copies of the *Beano*.

PHILIP REEVE

worked in a bookshop for many years before breaking out and becoming an illustrator. He is also the award-winning author of the *Mortal Engines* quartet. Philip now lives on Dartmoor with his wife, Sarah, and their son Samuel.

Urgum's back! In an adventure packed with yet MORE bizarre creatures, barbarians in bridal gowns, evil villainous budgies ... and some LEGENDARY underwear.

You'll laugh till you fall over!

Where there's trouble, there's Buster ...

Buster longs for a quiet life, but weird stuff just keeps happening in Smogley ...

The alien super-cabbages are coming and guess who's got to stop them ...?

WHERE THERE'S TROUBLE, THERE'S BUSTER ...

Buster longs for a quiet life, but weird stuff just keeps happening in Smogley ...

Buster doesn't have time to save the world from rampaging ice-freaks – they're spoiling a perfectly good summer holiday by invading!

Where there's trouble, there's Buster ...

Buster longs for a quiet life, but weird stuff just keeps happening in Smogley ...

There's a giant crazy hamster -
- and it's coming straight for Buster!